KISS ME, COWBOY

Cowboy Dreamin' 6

Sandy Sullivan

Erotic Romance

Secret Cravings Publishing
www.secretcravingspublishing.com

A Secret Cravings Publishing Book
Erotic Romance

Kiss Me, Cowboy
Copyright © 2014 Sandy Sullivan
Print ISBN: 978-1-63105-493-8

First E-book Publication: October 2014
First Print Publication: January 2015

Cover design by Dawné Dominique
Edited by Stephanie Balistreri
Proofread by Sarah Biggs
All cover art and logo copyright © 2014 by Secret
Cravings Publishing

PUBLISHER
Secret Cravings Publishing
www.secretcravingspublishing.com

Dedication

This is dedicated to Maranda.
Thank you for all you do for me as my personal
assistant. I don't know what I would do without you.
Jackson is next!

Lyn.
Love you!
Sandy
Sullivan

Kiss Me, Cowboy

Cowboy Dreamin' 6

Sandy Sullivan

Chapter One

Joshua Young brought the bottle of beer to his lips, to wash away the grime from a day in the saddle on his family ranch. *Damn, I'm beat.* A couple of his friends played pool in the corner as he watched with disinterest. He didn't care much for getting rambunctious tonight. The feeling of restlessness had him in its grip without showing signs of letting up. Maybe a raunchy night of sex would take care of his problem.

He glanced around the bar. A couple of his brothers sat with their girls in a corner booth. It was the first time his triplet, Joel, had been able to get Mesa out of the house since the birth of their little girl a few months before. He was happy for the brothers who'd hooked up with a woman recently. He actually felt it might be time for him to settle down. Jeff had his girl Terri, Joel had Mesa, Jeremiah had a special girl named Callinda, Jacob had Paige and now his other triplet Jason had hooked up with Peyton, one of the bartenders at The Dusty Boot. All of his brothers seemed to be pairing off...Okay, well not all of them. Jackson didn't have a steady girl, neither did Joey or Jonathan, but he started to think he'd be the last to find a woman of his own. He wasn't necessarily looking, but if he found her, then so be it. His plans were at the forefront of his thoughts.

Little did his family know, but he had a plan to make a lot of money to start his own business. He knew his parents would help him if he asked, but he wanted to do this on his own. Of course, he'd never been anything but a cowboy which meant it had to be something along those lines. His specialty was working with leather. With that, he planned to start his own saddlery.

He grabbed his beer and headed for the bar, tipping the bottle to his lips to empty the last dregs of the brew. Another one sounded good tonight, even though he didn't usually drink a ton. Tomorrow came early, so he should probably limit it to two.

Just as he reached the bar, someone bumped into him, dumping cold liquid down his back. "Shit!" He spun around to see who spilled beer, probably, on him and found a woman, who barely reached his shoulder. She had the prettiest green eyes he'd ever seen. They seemed almost a little sad, or maybe lonely would be a better word, before shock at what she'd done had registered.

"Oh my God. I'm so sorry. Someone bumped into me. Are you all right?"

"I'm fine. A little beer never hurt anyone."

"It's really crowded in here."

"Yeah, this is a typical Friday night at The Dusty Boot though." Intrigued, he tilted his head to the side to get a better look at her. "You new here?"

"Sort of." She pressed her lips together, drawing his gaze to the peach colored gloss on the pouty surfaces. "I'm really sorry," she shouted as the band started playing again.

"What?"

She leaned in close enough to be heard, bringing the scent of something fresh to his nose. "I said I'm really sorry for the beer down your shirt."

"Oh. It's okay. I needed a beer bath tonight."

She laughed, a little giggling sound, as she pressed her fingertips to her lips.

"I'm Joshua."

"I'm Candace."

She held out her hand for him. When he grasped it in his, her hold was firm and strong, not like most women he knew with a wimpy handshake. A tingle shot up his arm to warm something in his chest. "Nice name."

"Thank you. Yours too."

"You don't live around here."

"No. Actually, I live in California. I'm here visiting a friend who lives here."

"Welcome to Texas."

She smiled, showing off straight, white teeth and a small dimple in her left cheek. "Thank you."

"Can I buy you another beer?" he asked, stuffing his hand in his front right pocket to pull out some money.

"Um, sure."

He turned around to signal for Peyton to bring him two more beers as the little lady stepped up beside him to let someone pass behind her. "If you want something else, let me know."

"No, beer is fine. I usually don't drink much, but I'm here on vacation, so I want to experience everything Texas has to offer."

"Everything, huh?"

Her gaze slid down his frame from the top of his black Stetson to the tip of his dirty cowboy boots. "Yep."

It just might be his lucky night after all if this pretty little thing wanted to experience his kind of Texas rodeo.

"Six bucks, Joshua," Peyton said over the twang of the guitar on stage. One eyebrow shot up when he handed one to Candace. "New friend?"

"Yeah, sort of."

"I'm Peyton." She held out her hand across the bar to Candace. "I'm his sister-in-law."

"Nice to meet you. Candace."

"You're new here."

Candace laughed. "Is it that obvious?"

"You don't have the Texas twang to your speech, plus I know just about everyone who comes in here regularly. You I haven't seen before."

"I'm visiting a friend."

"Nice." Peyton tapped the bar with her knuckle. "Welcome. Holler if you want another one."

Peyton moved off down the bar to help other patrons while Joshua turned left to face Candace. "You can have the stool if you like."

"Thanks." She glanced down at her feet, showing him the tips of typical cowboy boots. "My feet are killing me in these."

He laughed as she shrugged and slid her cute little bottom up on the stool with an audible sigh. "Better?"

"Oh, much."

With one elbow on the bar, he leaned a little closer to inhale the scent clinging to her hair. But she was a sweet thing. He told himself it was because he wanted to hear her, but in reality, he loved the way she smelled. "Where in California do you live?"

"Do you know California at all?"

"Just the major towns like Los Angeles, San Francisco, you know."

"I live on the outskirts of Los Angeles in a small town called Anaheim."

"Isn't Disneyland there?"

Her lips tilted up at the corners. "Yes."

"Who are you visiting here? I probably know them."

"Arnold Beesman."

Joshua frowned. He knew Arnold from school, tough guy who turned into a pretty mean S.O.B. if he knew right. At least, that's what the rumor was. The guy had been married once, and supposedly, he beat his wife. "Yeah, I know him."

"He was married to my sister."

"Your sister is Mary?"

"Yeah. Did you know her?"

"Not personally, but I'd seen her around town a time or two. She seemed like a nice girl."

"She was."

"What happened to her? I thought they divorced."

"They did. She moved home and died six months later."

"How did she die if you don't mind me askin'?"

"She committed suicide."

"I'm sorry. I didn't mean to bring up bad stuff."

"No, it's okay. She didn't want the divorce. Neither of them did. She thought he'd been cheating on her and left. She found out, after she moved home, all about his infidelity when the woman he'd apparently been with called to laugh at her because she'd broken up their marriage. Mary loved him something fierce, and he loved her."

"So why didn't they get back together if they didn't want the divorce in the first place?"

"By then, he'd married the bitch who broke them up because she said she was pregnant when she wasn't."

"I'm sorry."

"Thanks."

"Would you like to dance?"

"And lose my prime seat?" She laughed as she hopped down. "I'd love to."

She put her beer next to his on the bar top while he tapped the guy next to him. "Save our seat, would you?"

"Sure, Joshua."

"Someone you know?" she asked as he led her to the dance floor with her hand in his.

"I don't think there's anyone in here I don't know, grew up with, or hung out with on Saturday nights at the ranch."

"You own a ranch?"

He swung around to face her. The look in her eyes gave him pause, catching his breath in his throat when he reached for her. Her long red hair hung around her shoulders like a cloud. Her eyes sparkled like emeralds he'd seen once in a jewelry store window. She had a white blouse on, tied under her breasts, leaving her flat abdomen showing as her little denim skirt rode low on her hips. The blush on her cheeks gave her a rosy glow. He couldn't believe his luck in finding such a rose in amongst a bunch of daisies. Not that the women of Bandera were bad looking. He'd been with several over the years, but Candace definitely stood out. He'd have to keep her close to his side if he wanted to see where the night might lead.

"I don't personally. My family has a cattle ranch slash guest ranch on the outskirts of town," he replied when they reached an empty spot on the hardwood. "Did you come with Arnold?" He slipped his hand onto her waist and took her left hand in his right as they started swaying to the music.

"Yeah. He's shooting pool with some guys near the back."

"You aren't into watching guys play pool?"

"Not really. I was enjoying the music when I dumped the beer down your back."

"Do you know how to two-step?"

"No."

"Follow me. Slide, shuffle, slide, slide. It's easy." She looked down at her feet as she tried to follow his steps. "Relax. I don't bite…hard."

Her head snapped up as she grinned. "Do you like sex?"

He stumbled with his steps.

"Gotcha."

He liked her. She had spunk and seemed a little crazy to boot. "I sure do. How about you?"

"Love it. Something about a man going down on me just revs my engine."

"Does it now?"

"Yep." One eyebrow shot up over her left eye. "Do you like going down on a woman?"

"I can't believe we are havin' this conversation."

"Shy?"

"No, but I'm not used to a woman being quite so bold about her sex life."

Leaning in, she tipped her head back to look up into his face. "I like bold men."

"How long you here for?" A man could drown in her eyes if he let himself. Her mouth would reach his should he so chose to bring their lips together.

"A month." She ran her tongue up under his chin until he gave into the temptation and brought his down so their mouths hovered bare inches apart. "Why?"

"I can see us havin' one hell of a good time while you're here. What do you say?"

She shook her hand free of his, sliding both up his chest to wrap around his neck. "Oh, I'd like that."

Her tangy breath whispered over his lips, bringing the thought of them wrapped around his cock tight enough to make him explode. "A bit wild, aren't you?"

"I'm here to have a good time, and by all that's holy, I'm going to have one." She glanced up at him through her lashes. "Now, it can be with you, cowboy, or someone else in this bar."

He felt sweat bead up on his upper lip. This girl was hotter than a branding iron ready to burn through cowhide, but he was ready to jump into this fire with both balls dangling over the hot poker. "Babe, I'm all ready for a wild ride with you."

"Good. We're on the same page then."

"When?"

"Let's dance a bit first. I'll let you know when." She pushed herself up against his chest as he settled his hands on her hips.

When her hips swayed from side to side, he about came in his pants. She kept rubbing herself against his now straining cock. If they walked off the dance floor, everyone would see how fucking horny he was.

"A little horny, cowboy?"

"A lot horny, babe. You've got me wound tighter than the springs on my truck." He rubbed his lips against her neck. "If we don't leave soon, I'm going to lose it right here on the dance floor."

"Ah, poor baby."

Joshua felt his arm almost ripped from the socket as Arnold shoved him back. "What the hell do you think you're doing?"

"Stop it, Arnold."

"You keep your pretty little ass away from him."

"I can dance with whomever I want to. You aren't my father."

"No, but I'm as close to a brother you've got here, Candace. These boys aren't your type."

She backed up and threw up her hands in disgust. "What's my type? You don't even know. I'm here visiting. It doesn't mean you can tell me who I can or cannot fuck."

"You ain't fuckin' nobody. I promised your sister to take care of you if you ever came out here and by damn, I plan to." Arnold moved toward her. "Candy, honey, getting hooked up with one of the Young boys is a bad idea all the way around."

"Look, Arnold. I'm not trying to just get in her pants. I'd like to get to know her," Joshua said, glancing around at the group beginning to form around them. He didn't like scenes, but this was turning into one fast. He needed to defuse the situation or he would be cock-blocked before the end of the evening. He could just feel the whole thing slipping out of his fingers.

Candace jammed her hands on her hips. "I want your cock, cowboy, not your heart."

A few people behind her snickered. It wasn't like the Young brothers to not have a woman to go home with. She wanted him. He wanted her. What the hell was the problem?

"You need to stop with this talk, Candy. Watch your mouth, young lady."

"I'm twenty-three years old, Arnold. I can talk how I want to, I can fuck who I want to, and I can live my life how I want to. If this is going to be a problem for you, then I'll just go back to Los Angeles now and forget this visit."

"No. I don't want you to go home. You're all I have left of Mary."

"Then stop trying to be a big brother."

"I can't."

"Then we have nothing more to talk about. I'll be on the first plane out of San Antonio tomorrow." The crowd parted like the red sea as she spun on her heels, heading for the front door.

Intending to go with her, Joshua stepped toward where she'd disappeared.

"Let her go, Young. She's too good for you," Arnold snapped, following in her wake.

Joshua stopped, turned and headed toward a stool and that long mahogany bar that would bring him some relief from his pent up frustrations with a whole lot of alcohol. He hadn't originally planned to get drunk tonight, but things changed when the little piece of fluff twisted his balls into a knot and left him hanging for the evening. Bitch of it was, he didn't want anyone else.

He needed another beer. His cock ached from need, and now that the woman who had him turned inside out had left for the night, he needed something to soothe his frazzled nerves before he headed home. Tonight would be a blue balls night for sure. None of the women in Bandera stacked up to the beauty who just walked out of his life.

* * * *

"Candy, wait."

"I'm done with this, Arnold. Leave me alone," she said, stopping next to her car to unlock it. "I didn't come here so you could run my life for me. I came to visit. Out of guilt or whatever, I don't know, but I wanted to see how you were. I can see you're just fine. I'm going home."

"Stay please? You mean the world to me, Candy. I don't want you to walk out of my life. I need you to remind me what an ass I am for letting Mary leave me."

With both hands braced on the top edge of her car, she said, "You aren't an ass for letting her leave, Arnold. You're an ass for cheating on her in the first damn place. No use wailing over it. You divorced and remarried. She committed suicide because she couldn't have you anymore and that pushed her over the edge. Why she took things to that extreme, I don't know, but she did. It's over."

"I need to protect you. For her. For Mary."

"No, you don't. I'm a big girl. I can take care of myself, especially where men are concerned. If I want to fuck the entire bar, then so be it. You have nothing to say about it."

He spread his hands out to his sides, imploring her to forgive him for his stupidity. "All right. I'm sorry. I shouldn't have butted in, but you don't want to hook up with one of the Young boys."

"And why not? He seemed like a nice guy. Built. Rugged. Good looking. Just the type I needed tonight."

"He'll use you."

She threw up her hands as she started to pace near the side of her car. "I want to use him. Backward. Forward. Doggie-style. Up the ass. Hell, I don't care, Arnold. Don't you understand? It's a quick fling. Nothing more. I don't need the complication of a man in my life. I just wanted to fuck a guy."

"Don't talk like that, Candy. You're innocent and good. You shouldn't be having sex."

"I'm old enough to know what I want. I'm not a damned virgin, Arnold. Trust me."

"You should be then."

"Stop acting the fool. I just want some down and dirty sex for the evening."

"Fine! Do what you want, but I won't help you pick up a man, and stay away from Joshua Young."

"Whatever. I'm done for tonight. The mystique is gone. I don't want anything to do with a man now. I just want sleep. The plane ride from Los Angeles was a long one. Let's just go home."

"Good. I'm glad you're thinking straight now." He opened his own truck sitting next to her car as she climbed inside hers and slammed the door.

Frustrating fucking man! I want a little cock, not a boyfriend for God's sake!

She cranked the car's engine until it turned over with a rumble. The rental car wasn't anything fancy. It would do in a pinch, unlike her nice little sports car sitting in the airport parking lot at home. One thing she didn't have to worry about was money. Her mother's side of the family name came with old money. Her granddaddy built his fortune from the railroad industry a long time ago, but they didn't flaunt their millions. The whole family worked for what they had.

The family fortune was an issue between Arnold and Mary for a long time. He hated the fact that she could just whip out her credit card and pay for anything. She didn't though. They lived on his income from working on cars. Mary had loved her life with her husband, until the day she'd found out he cheated.

Sure, all the kids got a lump sum when they turned thirty, never mind the fact Candace had a degree in business and ran her own company working with computer programs. This month-long vacation was her chance to cut loose, find a cowboy for the short go around, and live her life before she settled back into the everyday grind at her office. *Is there something wrong with just wanting sex? I don't think so, but maybe I'm wrong. What if something were to happen? What if I got pregnant or caught some disease?* "Stupid, Candace. He was a nice guy. Cute too."

She put the car into drive and followed Arnold out of the bar parking lot. *Oh well, my chance at Joshua Young is gone. If I don't give up and go back to Los Angeles tomorrow, I'd probably never see him again anyway.*

Chapter Two

As predicted, morning came bright and early on the ranch, no matter how much Joshua had drank the night before.

He groaned as he rolled over in bed when his alarm went off. It was his turn to take the guests out on their ride through the hills and valleys of Thunder Ridge Ranch. Most of the time, he loved having the guests here, but this morning wasn't one of them.

After the woman of his fantasies walked out of the bar the night before, he'd drank himself into a stupor. He didn't want to think about going home without getting laid, and no one else in the bar piqued his libido like the red-haired beauty he'd had the chance to hold for way too short of a time. He wanted more, much more, but she'd left without returning to take care of his problem. *Damn bad luck!*

The minute he sat up on the side of the bed, his stomach began to lurch. It wouldn't do any good to be sick. Jeff wouldn't care. Besides, his brother had seen him stagger into the main lodge as he checked the buildings before retiring, so Jeff would know he was drunk off his ass when he'd come in.

"Joshua?"

"Yeah, Dad?"

"Are you up? You have a group waiting at the barn."

"Yeah. I'll be there in a minute."

"I'll tell them."

He heard the front door on the lodge bang shut a few minutes later as the sounds of a couple arguing reached him through the wall. He strained to hear the voices, but they were muffled to his ears. He shrugged and bent over to grab his jeans from the floor. Hearing voices in the main part of the house wasn't unusual. The ghost couple they had living near his rooms in the upstairs part of the lodge kept him awake sometimes until they would finally quiet down and fade into the night. It was strange to hear them in the early morning hours though. They didn't make a lot of noise during the day, just at night.

With the clean T-shirt in his hands that he'd found in a dresser drawer moments earlier, he shrugged into the sweet-smelling, cotton material. He needed to get his ass moving. He might not even have time for a cup of coffee before he had to deal with tourists. His own fault, he knew.

The front door of the lodge banged shut again. "Joshua?"

Jeff.

"I'm coming. Be down in a minute. I'm putting my boots on right now."

What a pain in the ass this was turning into. This living at the main lodge sucked. Maybe it was time for him to get a place of his own.

As soon as he shoved his feet into his boots, he grabbed his straw cowboy hat from the end of his bed and opened the door. The faint odor of flowers drifted to his nose, telling him one of the female ghosts was nearby. "Go on now. I have work to do." He felt the brush of fingertips down his arm for a second before the scent disappeared. He knew one of the female ghosts liked him. She touched him often, but today wasn't a day for lollygagging. He had a lot of work to get done and a woman to forget about.

He grabbed a to-go cup of coffee from the table the minute he reached the downstairs lobby area. They always had some strong brew going from the early morning hours until late at night. Thank goodness for the cowboy way.

When he reached the barn, he was surprised to see such a large group of riders ready to go out this early in the morning. Joey would have to accompany him on this ride since the group had more than ten riders. "Joey?"

"Yeah?"

"I need you to go this morning."

"All right. Let me get Jeremiah to come out and tend the remaining horses while we're gone." Joey disappeared into the house a few minutes later in order for his other brother to be pulled from the work he was doing in one of the offices.

Several minutes later, the two of them returned to the barn. "We've got fifteen riders."

"Should I grab Jonathan?" Joshua asked, adjusting his hat on his head.

"No, we should be fine with us. The group doesn't have any new riders. They all have experience."

"Good. Let's get this over with. I need to get busy doing other chores."

"You okay?" Joey asked when they stepped into the corral with Jeremiah on their heels.

"Yeah, you look kinda green, brother." Jeremiah laughed because he knew Joshua was still hung over from the night before. He'd been watching from his seat next to Callie at the table where all the brothers with girlfriends had taken up residence.

"Kiss my ass, Jeremiah. You know damned well what went down last night."

"A distinctive case of blue balls, I think."

"Fuck you," he growled under his breath to keep the guests from hearing him as they approached. "Who needs help mounting?"

The rest of the morning was spent taking several groups out for hourly rides, grooming the horses, feeding, watering, and just general ranch work. It kept his mind off Candace even though he wished he knew if he'd see her again. *Maybe I can get Arnold's number from the phone book and call there. Nah, too forward.*

He contemplated the idea off and on all day long until the sun finally started to go down. The day had been completed. He could finally take some Tylenol and hit his bed early even though it was a Saturday night. His usual bar hopping would have to wait until his stomach settled down or he died, one or the other.

Car lights came up the driveway, heading for the main lodge.

He really didn't want to deal with guests tonight, so he walked toward the house hoping to avoid the newest arrivals. Just as he got to the door, his mother pushed it open, balancing on her crutches. "Oh Joshua, can you see to the new guest's luggage? She's arriving late and just wanted to settle into her room for the night."

"Uh, sure, Mom." He grumbled to himself as he turned back toward the waiting car. "God, *please* just let me die. I knew I shouldn't have hit those shots of tequila after I drank six beers, but I just needed to forget the ache in my—"

"Joshua?"

"Candace?"

* * * *

"What are you doing here?"

"I asked around town about you, and this is where they pointed me to."

"I thought you were going back to Los Angeles today?"

"I gave Arnold a choice. Stay out of my business or else."

Joshua laughed, the sound rumbling deep in his chest as he came closer. She liked it. The hearty, low laughter fit him perfectly. Those crystal clear, blue eyes reflected the light coming from the house. His hair hung a little longer than she normally liked on a guy, but the little scruff of five o'clock shadow had her humming her appreciation. She liked a man with muscles. Boy, did he have some all over. His biceps bulged from long days wrestling cattle. His chest looked sculpted and hard from throwing hay or some such cowboy thing. She just knew he was the real thing when someone mentioned cowboy.

"I'm glad you came to find me."

"I'm glad too."

"Are you staying at the ranch?" he asked, stuffing his hands in his front pockets.

"For a couple of days. I needed to get away from Arnold if you and I were going to…you know."

"Fuck?"

"Yeah," she replied, heat flaming her cheeks. How could she be embarrassed now after the bold way she talked the night before? It had been the alcohol talking. She probably shouldn't have had those two shots of whiskey between the beers. It was a good thing she hadn't been stopped on the short trip back to Arnold's, otherwise she'd probably have been arrested for DUI.

"What's wrong?"

She lowered her eyes. "Nothing."

He stepped in front of her and brought her chin up with a finger beneath it. "You're embarrassed by crass talk? You weren't last night."

"I had a bit too much to drink last night."

He pulled his hat off and pushed his fingers through his hair. "Yeah, me too. I'm a bit hung over today."

"Me too."

"How about we save the fucking for when we both feel better?"

"I'd like that."

He wrapped an arm around her shoulder in a hug, pulling her into his chest for a minute. "Good. I would too." After he stepped back, he moved around to the back of her car. "Pop the trunk, and I'll get your bag so we can get you registered."

Once she got the back of the car open, she stuffed the keys in her bag before she shut the trunk. "Thank you."

She fell into step beside him as they took the gravel walkway toward the front of the huge main building. A soft, warm glow illuminated the front walk of the house and the rockers set along the front porch. Several antique items graced the long expanse as well, including an old wringer washing machine, an antique ice box and what looked like a piece of an old plow. The whole building looked like something out of an old western movie. She loved it.

"No problem. My mom is waiting for you inside. I'm assuming you were her last minute guest she sent me out to help."

"Your mom?"

"Yeah. You'll love her. She's a great lady."

When Joshua pulled open the door, they ran smack into Jason and Peyton walking out. "Oh hey, bro."

Her mouth fell open in a soft oh as she looked at Jason and back to Joshua.

Joshua explained, "We're two of a set of identical triplets. You'll meet Joel at some point too."

"Triplets?"

"Yes."

"Wow."

"Yeah, a lot of people say that." He pointed to his brother and said, "This is Jason and his wife, Peyton. You met her at the bar last night."

"Oh yeah. Nice to see you again. It's Candace, right?"

"Yes."

"A friend of Arnold's?"

"Right again. He's my ex brother-in-law."

"Mary is your sister?" Jason asked, sliding an arm around Peyton's shoulder. "I remember her. Nice lady."

"Yes, she was."

"Was?"

"She committed suicide about a year ago."

"Oh my. I'm so sorry," Peyton said, squeezing her fingers. "If you want to talk while you're here, I'd be glad to listen."

"Peyton's is finishing up her degree in counseling," Jason said.

"That's awesome." Candace shuffled her feet a little as she glanced down. She wasn't really comfortable talking about her sister and what happened outside of telling people she committed suicide. The whole thing still left a bitter taste in her mouth.

"It's okay if you don't want to. I just thought I'd offer since I've been there myself."

"You have?"

"There were times I thought of suicide, yes. During the emotional abuse I suffered, there were plenty of times I wanted to end it all with a bullet or something, but I couldn't bring myself to do it. I knew there was something better for me out there." She leaned into her husband's embrace. "And I found it right under my nose at The Dusty Boot."

"I love you."

"I love you too, Jason. You're my life."

"Okay. Enough. Gag. Sputter. Spit."

"Oh hush, Joshua. You'll be there someday. Just wait."

Jason and Peyton laughed as they headed out the door. "You two have fun."

"We will," Joshua answered when the door closed behind them, and he ushered Candace through what appeared to be a large dining room. Several large picnic tables lined the walls. A long serving buffet sat off to one side where they served the meals. A huge coffee pot sat on a table between two openings that led into the main room of the ranch. "This is where we take meals. There will be a bell rung when it's time to eat. Breakfast is at eight. Lunch at noon and dinner at six."

They approached an office set back in the corner of the large room. To her left, out of the corner of her eye, she saw a cowboy sitting on one of the long leather couches near the fireplace. When she turned to get a better look, there wasn't anyone there. *Weird.*

A strikingly beautiful woman hobbled out on crutches as they approached, with her hand extended. Her long dark hair hung to the middle of her back in an inky cloud. Her features where close to Joshua's although Candace assumed he shared some other striking resemblance to his father. "You must be Candace. I'm Nina. My husband James and I are the parents of this brood of men."

"Ah. It's nice to meet you."

"You too. I have your room all ready. It's here in the main lodge. Joshua can show you up there. I just need your credit card."

"Sure." Shaking her head, Candace pulled out her wallet to hand Nina the card.

"Something wrong?"

"No. I guess not." She extended her arm toward Nina with her credit card between her fingers. "I just thought I saw someone sitting on the couch over there, but now there isn't anyone there."

"Oh. That's one of our resident ghosts. He's here a lot. Pay him no mind."

Nina went inside the office to run her credit card while Candace glanced at Joshua. "Ghost?"

"Yeah. We have a few. Him. A couple who hangs out upstairs and some kids who make noise in the yard."

"And I'm staying upstairs where these hang out?"

"I can have Mom give you one of the cabin rooms. They're usually quieter."

"No. I'm okay." She shivered a little at the thought of ghosts running around the property willy-nilly. "I think."

"You'll be just down the hall from Joshua's room in two-eleven."

"Great."

"I'll show you where it is so I can take your bag up there."

"I appreciate it."

"Did he tell you when breakfast is?"

"Yes, ma'am."

"Good. Thanks, Joshua," Nina said, closing the office door behind her as she got ready to leave for the night, hobbling on her crutches a few feet. "Coffee is always on down here if you find yourself an early riser or need a cup before bed. There is water for tea too."

She smiled, thinking how lovely this family turned out to be. Joshua had a great home life, it sounded like. "Thank you. You've been such a gracious hostess."

"Oh, you're welcome, dear. Just make sure to lock your door when you retire and ignore any sounds you hear up there during the night. Sometimes they get a little rowdy."

"I will. I have an iPod. I can play some soft music to drown out the sounds if I need to."

"If you hear arguing, that's them. They usually quiet down before midnight though. Did Joshua tell you this used to be a brothel?"

"A brothel? Wow. No, he didn't tell me."

"I was going to give you the tour tomorrow since I'm off."

"That would be fantastic. I'd love to get the whole cowboy feel."

"We have a pool, some horseshoe pits and lots of other things for guests to do. Make sure he shows you everything."

"Oh, I plan to."

"Night, kids." Nina waved as she moved slowly toward the long hall that lead to their personal quarters.

"Come on. I'll show you to your room."

"Will you join me?"

"I thought we agreed not tonight?"

She shrugged as she glanced at the floor. "I wouldn't mind just having you hold me. Being single really sucks sometimes for that one and one feel, you know."

He stopped her with a hand on her arm. "Listen, Candace. Girlfriends are great, but you don't live here. It's not like anything can come of a relationship between us."

With a sigh, she glanced up at him, realizing just how tall he stood compared to her five-something frame. "I'm not looking for a relationship, Joshua. Living in Los Angeles would be conducive to any kind of relationship anyway, even if I wanted one. I don't plan on moving. I have a life there. A business. My family."

"Okay. I just want to make sure we're on the same page, darlin'. If you want to have a good time for the timeframe you're here, I'm all for that."

"Sounds good to me."

They walked up the wooden stairs to the first landing. "There are rooms down this hall, but yours is on the next level."

"Where do the ghosts hang out?"

"On the second floor and third floor landing usually."

"Oh, goody."

"I can change your room if you like. Mom wouldn't mind."

"No, it's fine, but I might end up in your room for the night just so I can sleep. I'm not real fond of ghosts."

He smiled. "They don't hurt anything. It's a residual thing. They argue, you hear some crashing glass and then it stops usually. It only goes on once or twice a night."

"Great." She rolled her eyes as they reached the second floor.

"Your room is at the end of the hall."

"Where is yours?"

"Two doors down from yours."

Tilting her head to the side, she looked him up and down. She really wanted him in her bed tonight, but it probably wasn't a good idea since they both felt like shit. She could really use some sex though. She might just have to dig out B.O.B.

"What are you thinking?" he asked, opening her door and putting her suitcase on the bed.

"How much I want you in my bed."

"How much?"

"A lot, cowboy."

"Good because I want to be there too." He pushed his fingers into the hair at her temple as he lowered his head.

"Do you masturbate?"

Her question snapped his head back in shock.

He choked a bit before he answered, "Sometimes."

She thought the red stain on his cheeks was cute. He really did blush. "Me too, and baby, I plan to masturbate to the look in your eyes when you look at me. You want me. Bad."

"You really are kind of bold, aren't you?"

She raked a fingernail down his chest before she fiddled with a button on the front of his shirt, debating on whether to undo it and lick the skin beneath. "When

I know what I want, I go after it. I want you. Right now."

He took her hand in his, stopping her movement. "Tomorrow night. It's a date." He leaned in and kissed her on the nose. "Sleep well."

"Party pooper."

The grin he flashed her curled her toes. The man truly had it all. Tall, dark, handsome, big blue eyes, hair peeking out from under the cowboy hat, tight western shirt across his broad chest and Wrangler jeans just tight enough to make her mouth water. She wondered what the scruff on his face would feel like on the sensitive skin of her inner thighs. She hoped tomorrow, she'd find out.

"You'll survive the night, darlin', and then tomorrow evenin', I'll rock your world."

"Is that a promise?"

"You bet."

"I'm holding you to it."

"I'll see you in the mornin'."

"Night, cowboy."

"Goodnight."

Chapter Three

Used to being up at the crack of dawn, Joshua rolled out of bed at daybreak even though he'd had a rough night. Horny didn't adequately describe his state of affairs after Candace ran her fingernails down his chest. The shivers that had raced down his body mystified him. He'd never reacted to a woman so strongly before, not anyone around Bandera anyway. He'd been to bed with a few of the single ladies in town, but they didn't trip his trigger the way Candace did with merely a touch.

Oh well. He'd play it for what it was worth. She wasn't a local girl. Worrying about her getting all tied up in him the way some women around here played it wouldn't be a problem. Many of them wanted the Young name and what they thought was a lucrative business in their ranch. Little did they know, the place wasn't making millions. They did okay and managed to survive from year to year, but as the boys kept adding to the family herd, things got tighter and tighter.

A moment later, he stood in front of the bathroom mirror in his jeans, tilting his head from left to right, examining the five o'clock shadow on his chin and cheeks. He really hated shaving most mornings. It seemed to be the bane of his existence with the dark hair. Dark chest hair sprinkled across his pecs while a thin line trailed toward his groin. Some women liked that little happy trail. He shrugged. He wondered if Candace liked to go down on a man.

Eating pussy was one of his favorite past times, so he couldn't quite understand when a man didn't want to do that for a woman. They sure seemed to like it when he did it. A chuckle escaped him as he ran his right hand over his cheek. He slathered shaving cream across the surface in preparation to shave the stubble from his face. Whisker burn on a creamy white surface made him smile as he lost himself in thoughts of Candace with her pretty thighs wrapped around his head.

When he'd finished raking the razor over his face, he smoothed his hand over the surface to check for residual stubble left behind. He'd probably have to shave again before their resounding bout of sex tonight so he wouldn't scrape her up with it, but he'd leave that for later. He had plans to wine and dine her today with a picnic, horseback riding, and lots of making out before tonight. He wanted her hot and ready for him when they got around to making the bedsprings squeak.

A small knock on the door spun him around. Who could be there this time of morning? It wasn't even breakfast time yet.

He opened the door a moment later to find Candace dressed in a form fitting pair of jeans, white blouse and cowboy boots.

"I'm glad you're up. How about a sunrise horseback ride?" she asked, leaning against the door frame with her arms crossed under her impressive breasts.

The thought of burying his face between them and licking her pert little nipples had him hard in a flash. Horseback riding would be interesting with a hard-on. "Sure. Have you had coffee yet?"

"Yep. I've been downstairs, drank a cup, did some work on my laptop, and fed the donkeys."

"Wow. Are you always an early riser? I didn't think you'd be up yet."

"I'm usually at work by six in the morning at home. Running your own business is a twenty-four hour job."

"I imagine," he said, slipping on his shirt while she watched. He really did like the look in her eyes when she ran her gaze over his frame. "For us it is. We have guests arriving all hours of the night. Entertaining some of the guests is a big job."

"Does each of you have a specific one to do around the place?"

"Not so much. A few of us do, like Joey handles the new horses. Jeff acts as the foreman of the ranch. Jonathan handles the website and marketing stuff. Jeremiah is the financial planner. He handles our investments and whatnot." He sat on the bed for a moment to slip on his boots. Nothing compared to a well-made pair of cowboy boots, in his mind. Comfort and fit made all the difference in the world. He glanced down at the boots on her feet. They looked brand new. "Did you buy boots in town before you came out here?"

Pink stained her cheeks when she blushed. The tips of the boots bounced up and down slightly as she wiggled her toes in them. "Does it show that much?"

"They look new is all."

"Not like yours."

"I wear mine every day so yeah, there is a difference between my worn ones and your new ones."

"I needed to be the quintessential cowgirl when I came out here. I figured you liked that kind of woman."

He brushed his fingertips across her cheek. "I like you just the way you are. Cowgirls are great, but I don't have to have one to be happy."

"What kind of woman do you like?"

"Your kind."

The smile spreading across her lips lit up the room. It obviously didn't take a lot to make her happy. He frowned, wondering what kind of life she led that the smallest compliment would light up her world.

"Shall we get some coffee?"

She laughed. "I've already had some."

"Would you like another cup? I can't function without having a cup of java before I start the day." He pulled the door shut behind him before they headed down the hall to the stairs. "I hope the ghosts didn't keep you up last night. I don't hear them much anymore since I'm used to it now."

"I heard them for a little bit, but like your mother said, they quieted down before midnight. I worked on some stuff on my laptop. When I heard the noises, I listened for a bit, then went to bed."

"Hear anything interesting?"

"Nothing more than you told me. They argued a bit. I heard something break, and then they stopped." They reached the landing at the bottom of the stairs and headed toward the coffee pot. "It wasn't too bad. It's interesting to hear it though. I couldn't make out the words, just murmuring of an argument."

"You heard the majority of it then."

"Have you ever done more research on the place to see if you could find out who they are?"

"Not really. We know the place was a working cattle ranch way back when and later a brothel when the family lost the ranch to the bank. We think the kids were from the ranch heyday. The cowboy too, but we figure the couple was one of the call girls who worked here when it was a brothel."

"They could be the ranch owner and his wife too."

He nodded in acceptance of her thought. "True."

"It would be interesting to know the background."

"We take the ghosts with a grain of salt. They are here and don't interact much, except the cowboy."

"He does?"

Joshua put his cup beneath the spout on the coffee pot to pour the pungent brew. Coffee was his life's blood sometimes when he'd had a hard night. "Yeah. He answers good mornin' when you say it to him or tips his hat when he's seen, but nothing much more than that." Interesting how she'd taken to wanting to know more about the history of the place than even his parents.

"I think it would make a great documentary. You know how people like ghost stories, and if we caught it on video, that would be something. It would make your place famous."

"We don't want the weirdo ghost people out here sniffing around. We just like to do our thing and leave them to theirs."

Excitement surrounded her. "But you all could be rich. Don't you want more money than you could possibly spend?"

"Not really, no."

"I don't understand."

"Do you come from money, Candace?"

"Well, yeah, I guess you could say that. I grew up not wanting for anything, and I have a trust fund I'll get when I turn thirty."

He pushed his hat back on his head. "How much?"

"What?"

"How much is your trust fund?"

"Ten, but I don't see—"

"Ten what? Million, billion, thousand?"

"Million."

"I'm lucky to have twenty bucks in my pocket to party on during a Saturday night binge at The Dusty Boot. My parents raised us nine boys on this ranch without a silver spoon in our mouths. You don't know what it's like to have to work for your money."

"Yes I do, Joshua. I have my own company. I work from six in the morning to midnight most nights. I work my ass off for what I have."

He sipped his coffee, contemplating how to say what was on his mind without pissing her off. "But you have a trust fund to fall back on. I'm not knocking your way of life, but don't assume we all want what you have, darlin', because we don't. I like the simple life, my horses, the cattle, the sunsets, and sunrises over the hills of our ranch. This is my existence, and I like it this way."

She put her hand on his arm. "I can see how that kind of life would be appealing, but what about nice cars, boats, vacations?"

"I have everything I need right here."

"Let's just agree to disagree on this since I can't seem to convince you that having money isn't all that bad."

"I'm not sayin' it is, but you have to realize everything isn't about money. Love of family is an important part of my life, and I wouldn't change it."

"I love my family too."

"I'm sure you do."

"Why do I get the feeling you're patronizing me?" she asked, her hand on her hip although a smile played on her kissable lips.

She'd matched him word for word during their little disagreement. Her personality definitely said she was intelligent, spunky, and wouldn't back down in a fight. He wondered what the business she mentioned entailed. "I'm not patronizing you at all, darlin'." He brought the cup to his lips for a sip of the coffee as she did the same. "What type of business do you have?"

"I run a computer programming firm."

"So you know computers?"

She laughed. "I've known a few, yeah."

"You'll have great conversations with Jonathan then. He's our computer genius around here."

"Great. I'd like to talk shop with him while I'm here."

The workers started filing in to get breakfast ready which would be in about an hour. "Would you like to wait until after breakfast for our ride?"

"If you want to show me some other stuff around the ranch and then ride, that's fine with me."

"I want to give you the most for your money of the cowboy experience. Ridin', ropin', swimmin', four-wheelin', muddin'—"

She giggled. "What the hell is muddin'?"

"It's where we take our trucks through the huge mud puddle, throwing mud everywhere. It's a great time."

"Mud everywhere?"

"Yep."

"Sounds like fun."

"We usually have a bunch of people from town come out, have a bonfire, roast marshmallows. You know."

"Why don't you show me around the ranch while we wait for breakfast?"

"Sounds good." He tossed the dregs of his coffee into the trashcan as she did the same. He grasped her hand in his, wondering at the zing of spark shooting up his arm from her touch. Women weren't hard to come by when you were a cowboy to the bone. He was used to women coming onto him, but this one was a nice mixture of bold and shy at the same time. "What do you want to see first?"

"Whatever you want to show me."

They wandered around the ranch, checked out the gardens, the barns, walked up the trails a bit, went by the swimming pool, and then stopped at the rocking chairs on the front porch while the donkeys pestered them for goodies, until they heard the clang of the breakfast bell. "Shall we get some breakfast?"

"Yeah, I'm starving."

"Good. A girl who likes to eat. It bugs me when girls only eat a salad or some shit when I'm eating steak."

"Not me, buddy. I like my food."

He laughed as he held out a hand to help her to her feet and escorted her into the dining room. They crossed the main lodge meeting room, through the arched entry way into the dining room while the rest of the guests began filing in for food. He stopped at the family table to tell them he would be eating with Candace.

Once they grabbed their food, she found them a corner spot where they could sit and talk quietly. He knew the noise got to be pretty loud in there when they had big groups. Right now, it was off season so things were a bit slower. They still had a couple of families with some rambunctious kids.

He took the seat across from her to be able to look into her eyes. She had pretty eyes. The green almost reminded him of the junipers on the mountain, a deep forest green. They sparkled with mischief as he put a forkful of eggs into his mouth. "What?"

"You. I never thought I'd be spending time with a real cowboy on this trip. I figured I'd be stuck in Arnold's house watching television the whole time while he worked or something." She looked down at her plate before catching his gaze again. "Thank you."

"I haven't done anything yet, darlin'."

One perfectly arched eyebrow went up over her left eye. "Oh but you will, cowboy, you will."

* * * *

Candace couldn't believe how bold she was being with Joshua. She never acted this way, well almost never. She was usually the bookworm, nerdy type girl, who spent most of her time in the library in college, rather than partying with the girls who couldn't seem to go more than three months without sleeping with someone. Not her. She'd only had one serious boyfriend in her past, and she'd dumped him not too long ago. The creep had been using her for her money and name. She'd kicked him out when she caught him screwing one of her employees on a desk at work. They'd been dating for three years, and she thought she'd loved him. Apparently, he didn't love her though. She hadn't realized it until after she'd caught him cheating, that he'd been pulling away from her the minute he found out she didn't get her trust fund until she was thirty. He couldn't wait that long to start spending her money. She should have known though.

The signs had been there, everything from making her buy dinner when they went out to not paying his half of the rent for the last several months. She'd been used heartily. She wouldn't be used again. She planned to be the user in whatever situation now. "Are you up for the rodeo, cowboy?"

"Whatever you say, honey."

The minute they finished their meal, Joshua grabbed both their plates and took them to the dirty dish bin, while she finished her orange juice and walked the glass to the bin herself. "So what's first?" she asked, shoving her hands into her back pockets.

He swiped the hat from his head to brush some of the hair back before replacing it. "I thought we'd go for a ride up in the hills. I can show you the scenery while I check on the fences."

"I thought you were off today?"

"We never really have a day off, it seems. One day is a little less busy than the others is all." He glanced at her face and arms. "Do you have a hat?"

"No."

"Come on. Mom has some in the store you can purchase. You need one to protect your fair complexion in this Texas sun."

"I live in California. I'm in the sun all the time." She looked at her arms and the slight tan she sported. "I'll be okay."

"Trust me on this. You go pick out a hat while I get us a couple of bottles of water to take along. Even though it doesn't seem that hot right now, it could get pretty warm, even this late in the season."

A sharp exhale rushed from her mouth. "All right. I'll bow to your expertise on this since you live here and I don't."

"Good girl." He swatted her butt as she walked back into the main room and to the right to check out the assortment of cowboy hats in the small store.

There were tons of little knick-knacks, cowboy hats, decorations, cowboy things, and T-shirts. She found herself browsing through the selection of hats on the rack, trying on first one and then another before Joshua came in to find her. "Which one looks better? The one with the feathers down the back or the one with the gold hat band?"

"The feathers look more like something you would wear."

"This coming from the cowboy who noticed my brand new boots."

He smiled. "I'm very observant."

"You are, huh?"

"Yes, ma'am. I notice how you lick your lips when I get close, like this." He stepped near her, leaning in so his mouth was only a few inches from hers. "I see your eyes dilate. I can tell your nipples pebble the closer I get."

His breath fanned over her lips, making them ache for the touch of his.

"Your fingers are curled tight around the brim of that hat as the need to reach for me overwhelms you."

His scent surrounded her. Musk and male mixed with a woodsy smell reached her nose as her breathing increased tenfold.

He didn't touch her. He didn't have to. Her body went on high alert for this man the minute he'd turned around in the bar. She needed him, wanted him, would kill to have him kiss her right here, right now in the middle of his mom's shop. "Kiss me."

"Nope." He backed up, taking the hat from her hands and putting it on her head. "Two horses await us, ma'am, and anticipation is half the fun."

He pushed her out the door and around the corner so she could tell his mom to put the hat on her tab before they went outside to find the horses in the stable.

"Have you been on horseback before?"

"Once or twice. Nothing recently."

"I'll make sure to rub your sore spots then." They walked through the big doorway into the cooler interior of the tack room before he escorted her out the back door to where the horses were tied. Black, brown, spotted, gold colored, big ones, smaller ones and one huge red colored horse stood tied to the fences with water buckets near their feet. Each had a heavy leather saddle across their backs with a bulky blanket underneath. Some had metal bits in their mouths with one piece of leather over their ears while others only had what she remembered were called halters.

"Do you want a gentle horse?"

"That would probably be a good idea, although not a glue factory ready-made one, please."

His laughter burst from his lips in a gut-rolling explosion of guffaws. She liked his laugh and his smile. Hell, she liked him…a lot.

A moment later, he brought over a beautiful sorrel mare with a white blaze down her nose. "She's gorgeous!"

"Her name is Pearl."

The hair on the mare's nose felt soft when Candace ran her palm across the surface. "How are you, pretty girl?"

The horse nickered softly as if she answered in kind.

"Do you think you can mount or would you like to use the mounting block?"

"I think I could swing my big butt up there."

He waggled his eyebrows. "I could give you a boost."

"That would be mighty kind of you, sir." She did a little bobbing curtsy, sweeping her imaginary gown to the side. When he picked her up by the waist to plop her in the saddle, she let out a little squeal. "Thank you, kind sir."

He tipped his hat in that adorable cowboy way. "You're mighty welcome, ma'am."

The horse did a little sidestep, jostling her as she stared too hard. The view of Joshua hoisting himself into the saddle on another horse got her blood pumping. *Damn, he had a fine ass in those jeans. Wranglers. Country folks called them Wranglers and by damn I'm going to be country for the month I'm here.*

As Joshua led the way out of the corral, her horse voluntarily followed behind close enough she could see the breadth of his shoulders in his western style shirt, the strength of his hands when he grasped the reins in a relaxed grip and the bulge of his arms as he guided the horse around boulders in their path.

"Where are we going?" she asked, talking loudly in case he couldn't hear her from back where she followed behind.

He twisted around in the saddle a bit to talk to her. "To a little spot I know. You'll love it. There's a nice little pool where the stream comes down the mountain. The water is kind of cold, but you can dip your pretty little toes in it, so you can enjoy the bubbling stream."

"Sounds like heaven."

"It's a little piece of heaven here on Thunder Ridge. Us boys used to go down there in the summer and swim all the time."

"How far is it?"

"Not far. It'll take about half an hour to get there."

"What are all these trees?"

"Juniper."

"Isn't Texas known for bluebonnets?"

"Yes, but they come out in the spring. It's right pretty that time of year around here."

"I bet." They rode in silence for a bit. Her thighs had begun to hurt already from riding. She hoped they got to the pond soon otherwise her pussy wouldn't be up to having sex tonight with the hunky cowboy riding in front of her. "Are we almost there?"

"You're as bad as a kid asking are we there yet." He laughed.

The sound sent shivers down her arms. "Sorry. I haven't been on a horse in a long time."

"We haven't been riding that long."

"I'm still going to be walking bowlegged at this rate."

He chuckled again while they rounded a huge boulder. The scene before her took her breath away. A large pond surrounded by boulders spread out like a smorgasbord with flowers, junipers, and rocks scattered about. Water poured over the large rocks in a beautiful waterfall. "Wow."

"I knew you'd like it."

"This is gorgeous, Joshua. I can see why you wanted to come here."

"We don't get to visit it as much as we did when I was a kid, but I do try to come out here about once a week just to think. It's quiet."

He swung down from his saddle in the smoothest motion she could have imagined. She sighed when he tied his horse to a low hanging branch before he walked toward her in a natural cowboy swagger.

"Let me help you."

She got her leg over the saddle horn before he reached up with his big hands, wrapped them around her waist and swung her around. She slid down his torso. The fire burning in his gaze set her insides into an inferno of need. *Lordy.* She wanted to experience this man's touch more than her next breath. "Joshua," she whispered, holding a death grip on his biceps, afraid he would let her go, and she'd toppled into a heap on the ground at his feet, not that she would mind worshipping him like the god he was.

When her boots finally touched the ground, she realized just how much taller than her five-foot five-inch frame he stood. He had to be at least six foot three, she guessed when she looked up into the beautiful blue of his gaze. *What gorgeous eyes.*

"You are a beautiful woman."

"Uh, thanks."

"I could eat you up." He stepped back. "But I won't right now."

"Why the hell not?"

"It's not the right time." He chuckled again as he moved toward the pool to their right. "Anticipation."

"I'm anticipating throttling you if you don't touch me soon."

He glanced back over his shoulder with a crooked grin while he struggled to take one of his boots off. "You comin'?"

Chapter Four

"Not yet, cowboy."

The cocky grin returned. He got the other boot off, pulled off his socks and then rolled up his pant legs. "The water feels great. Come on."

She sighed heavily before moving to his side. She wanted to push his ass into the water or jump in herself to cool the burning in her pussy. The level of desire this man had her simmering at went beyond anything she'd experienced before. Heat boiled just below the surface of her skin.

"You okay? Your face is flush."

"I'm fine," she gritted out. She plopped down on the rock next to him, clenching her fists while she tried to keep from jumping him right there next to the pool.

"You don't look fine." He touched her cheeks with his palms. "You aren't hot."

"I'm not?"

"Well, you are in one sense of the word, but feverish, no." He reached over and pulled off her boots before her socks. "Put your feet in. It's really a nice temperature."

The cool water soothed her frazzled nerves. Jumping him seemed like a reckless thing to do, but man did she want him badly. "Thanks."

"For what?"

"Helping with my boots. The water does feel fabulous." He smiled that crooked little grin of his, tempting her to taste him from the gorgeous mouth to wherever she ended up last. "What are we going to do from here?"

"Fishing is out since we didn't bring poles." He tapped his fingers against his chin while he concentrated. "We have a lot more land you haven't seen. How about we ride some fence while we're out?"

"Okay." She didn't sound convinced even to herself.

"You wanted to experience everything cowboy, right?"

"Yeah, but I was thinking of other experiences."

"I plan to take you from city to country girl in the space of the month you're here. You will have everything country from the food, to ridin' horses, to muddin', to four-wheelin'."

"Sounds perfect."

He leaned back on the rock with his hands behind his head. His hat shaded his eyes from the sun, keeping her from seeing the gorgeous blue of his gaze. *Those eyes make me all gooey inside.* She wanted nothing more than to snuggle up to his side, rest her head on his tempting chest, and tick away the afternoon without a care in the world. It sounded like a little piece of heaven to her. Instead, she swished her feet around in the water, loving the feel of the cool wetness on her toes.

"Are those the things everyone likes to do for fun around here?"

He turned toward her, pushing his hat back so he could look at her. "Yep. Drinkin', dancin'. You know. All those kinds of thing. What do you city folk do for fun?"

She leaned back on her hands as she watched a bird flit from tree branch to tree branch across the pond. The sunlight reflected off the water, making it sparkle like diamonds in the sunlight. "We go out to the beach to listen to the water lap against the shoreline. Drive out to the mountains to go skiing. Go to the lake to water ski. Maybe go out to dinner at a nice restaurant, all dressed up in our best clothes. Have dinner parties at the house where everyone sits around drinking wine, talking, and laughing."

"Sounds kind of boring."

"No, not really. It's what we do."

"I think you'll like doing all the physical stuff we do our here. You look like a physical kind of girl."

"I do like to go hiking and swimming."

"Did you bring a bathing suit?"

"Of course."

"Are you wearing it now?"

"No." She glanced his way, wondering what he might be getting at.

"Too bad. I'd take you into the pond. It's deep enough to swim, but shallow enough to stand."

A thought crossed her mind and she giggled as she stood up. "Sounds good to me." She drew her T-shirt over her head and tossed it onto the rock next to him. Her bra came next, then her pants and underwear. "Last one in has to ride home in wet clothes." She jumped in, coming up for air in the center.

"Oh no you don't."

He quickly stripped out of his clothing, leaving nothing to her imagination. The man was gorgeous. His broad chest sprinkled with chest hair, took her breath away. The trim waist showed off a body the gods would weep for. A sexy little happy trail wound down his abdomen, showing off his six-pack abs to perfection. His biceps bulged with each movement while he worked his jeans off his legs. His long, thick cock bobbed against his stomach. Even partially aroused, the man had it going on in more ways than one.

"Wow," she whispered as she watched him slide into the pool of water.

He came up for air near where she stood in the middle of the pond. "This feels good. The heat seems to be climbing today."

"Yeah."

"Are you okay?"

"I'm great," she said breathlessly, not sure if it was because he was standing in front of her buck-ass naked or because of the cool water.

His fingers did a slow crawl up her arm to her shoulder, leaving goose bumps in their wake. "Are you sure you're okay? You look, I don't know, a little flustered."

"I am."

"Why," he whispered, leaning in to the point where his lips were almost touching hers.

She wanted him to kiss her. She needed him to touch her somewhere, anywhere. "Kiss me."

"My pleasure."

He softly brushed his lips against hers, a mere touch like butterfly wings softly whispering over her mouth. Everything tingled from the roots of her hair to her toes. She wanted more.

His tongue danced along the seam of her lips, asking her to allow him in. Should she? *What the hell.* She opened her mouth, giving him the access he wanted, letting him take this encounter to the next level. He pushed his tongue deep into her mouth with a soft moan. She titled her head to the side, allowing him to deepen the kiss to mind-blowing. Her hands settled on his shoulders while his snaked around her body, bringing her into full chest to breast contact.

The hair on his skin tickled the swell of her breast, pulling her nipples into tight, tingling nubs of pleasure. Her pussy throbbed with need to have him inside her, but he held back, only kissing her until she couldn't breathe without him surrounding her senses.

When his mouth left hers to slide from her lips to her ear, she sighed in contentment. She wrapped her arms around his neck, guiding his mouth lower.

The water lapped at her breasts just above her nipple line, giving him full access to her neck, shoulder and upper breast. His mouth skimmed over the surface, causing her to shiver in the wake of his assault on her skin. He nipped at her ear, the skin of her neck, then her shoulder while he made his way lower still.

His fingers made their way down her abdomen to dive between her parted thighs.

Yes!

One finger scraped along her clit, driving her up on her toes as his mouth closed over her left nipple to suck strongly.

A heavy moan escaped her lips. She wanted this, needed this. It had been a long time since she'd had sex, and never had a man driven her to distraction the way Joshua had.

"Please."

"Please what?" he asked around the flesh of her breast. "Please suck harder? Please finger-fuck me? Please touch me? You need to be more specific, Candace."

"All of the above?" She squirmed when the tip of his finger penetrated her pussy, giving her just a teasing of what was to come.

He took her nipple into his mouth, sucking hard enough he brought the tip to the roof and rubbed it with his tongue.

"Ah!" When his fingers pushed all the way inside her, the threadbare control with which she held onto her sanity slipped. "God, Joshua. I can't stand it. Make me come, please."

He lifted her into his arms and strolled toward the bank where their clothes lay. The rocks dug into her back when he laid her down on the sandy shoreline, but she didn't care. She wanted this more than anything.

"I'm not going to make love to you."

"What? Why the hell not?"

"Because I want to savor that moment in time with everything inside me. For now, I will worship your body with my mouth."

His lips skimmed over her breast, licking and nipping as he went farther down, across her abdomen until he was positioned between her thighs with her legs over his shoulders. At the first touch of his tongue to her aching clit, she almost came off the sand like a bottle rocket whizzing across the sky. Her body hummed with need so strong, she lost her mind when he shoved two fingers into her pussy again, sucking her clit between his lips not a second later.

When he curled his fingers up behind her pubic bone to hit that special spot, she flew apart on a cry of ecstasy with his name on her lips.

Her body slowly returned to a pre-orgasmic state as her heart rate decelerated and her breathing went back to normal. He crawled up beside her and wrapped her in his embrace as he laid back in the sand.

His cock lay hard against her hip. "I should help you out even if we aren't going to make love. You are hurting, I'm sure."

"Baby, it's okay. I'm good until we can find a bed, some cool sheets and a condom."

"You don't have one on you?"

He propped himself up on his elbow, his free hand skimmed from one breast to the other in a slow motion.

"No. I didn't plan on making love to you out here although it's pretty sexy how you came apart a minute ago."

He circled the nipple of her left breast with his fingers, curling her toes in the process. "Bummer."

"We have plenty of time."

"We should probably get dressed. What if one of your brothers comes out here?"

"They won't unless they are looking for me. I told Joey we were headed out here."

She ran a fingernail down his chest, swirling it in the hair lying there for a moment before she traveled farther down to his cock. "This is rather nice."

"I'm glad you like it."

"What kinds of things do you like when a woman goes down on you?"

"Let's see. Swirling her tongue around the head. Using her fingers to caress my balls while she's sucking. The whole warmth of her mouth around the shaft really does it for me, but it's the feeling of her fingers on my balls at the same time that will shoot me through the ceiling."

"I'll keep that in mind when I have a chance to wrap my mouth around your luscious cock."

His breath caught in his throat for a moment before he released it in a heavy sigh. "Sounds like a little piece of heaven to me."

"Oh, you'll think so before I'm done with you."

"How about we get dressed, head back to the ranch and get some lunch."

"Already?"

He picked up his watch from the pile of clothes. "Yep. It's almost eleven-thirty and by the time we dress and ride back, it'll be lunch time."

He raked his gaze down her body, heating her up with nothing more than the look in his eyes.

"After lunch we can find something else to do. Maybe four-wheelin'."

"Sounds good." She managed to sit up for a second before he pulled her back down for another toe-curling kiss.

"I needed that before we got dressed."

"Mmm. Me too."

The look in his eyes while he watched her put her clothes back on, told her he wanted her badly. When he shoved his still engorged cock into his jeans and zipped them up, her mouth watered to taste him, smell him and see where the afternoon would lead right there on the sandy shoreline. Alas, he didn't bring a condom, and she hadn't either. Love making would have to wait. No matter, she knew they would get there eventually. Anticipation might kill her before they did, but she could handle it if she had to. Right now, she had to.

As she sat on the rock to slip on her boots, she watched him do the same. It would be an uncomfortable ride back for him, she was sure. She shrugged. She'd offered to take care of his problem with or without a condom, but he wouldn't budge. He was careful. Too careful almost, making her consider what might've made him that way. Did he have a past love who'd wronged him? Maybe some women had given him some kind of disease. Or maybe gotten pregnant when he didn't want a child?

She really didn't know much about him. She probably should do some questioning before this went any further.

* * * *

They rode back toward the main lodge house almost in silence. Joshua had to wonder what she was thinking as they made their way around boulders and junipers. His cock throbbed behind the fly of his jeans. What the hell was he thinking not bringing a condom?

His horse stumbled, but regained his footing on the rocking ground. The gelding had pretty good footing most of the time. He would have to check and make sure the horse hadn't thrown a shoe while they'd ridden to the pond. "You're awful quiet back there."

"I'm thinking."

"About?"

"You. What makes you tick?"

"I'm just a simple cowboy."

"Did you always want to be a cowboy?"

"What else would I do with a family owning a ranch?"

"Surely there are other things in your life besides riding, roping, herding cattle, throwing hay, breaking horses, et cetera?"

He shrugged as he picked his way around another boulder. "Maybe."

"So what other things do you like to do?" she asked, sounding like she really wanted to know more about him.

"I work with leather."

"Doing what?"

"Making things like customized bridles and saddles."

"Wow. So you like to work with your hands, huh?"

"Yep."

"What else?"

"I like to drink beer, throw darts, and play pool."

"Well that's seems typical behavior for someone who hangs out at The Dusty Boot."

"I don't go there a lot. I usually spend my weekends working on my leather."

Silence enveloped them for a moment before she asked, "Ever had a serious relationship?"

"What do you mean by serious?"

"Have you been in love before?"

He paused, wondering how much to reveal. He hadn't really told anyone about *her*. "Yeah. Once. It was a girl I met in high school."

"What happened?"

"She found someone else more appealing."

"Seriously?"

"I don't like to talk about it."

"I can understand that. I mean really, how could someone think they could find someone more appealing than you?"

"You're good for my ego."

"Just speaking the truth. You're one sexy dude."

"You aren't just saying that because I gave you an orgasm, are you?" He laughed, letting her know he didn't think that was the case, but when his former love left because of a job, his ego had taken a beating. He wasn't sure when he would find the woman who would make all of the others disappear from his mind, but when he did, he would hold on with both hands. He glanced at Candace before he shook his head. Nope. She didn't live here. A relationship with her wouldn't work even if he thought she was pretty spectacular.

"No, I'm not saying that because you gave me an orgasm. I want to sample all your charms, Joshua, not just how wicked your tongue is."

They rode into the ranch corral with her last words reaching his ears and those of Joey and Jackson who stood nearby. *Damn.*

Jackson's eyebrow went up as a smile spread across his lips. Joey just laughed, taking the reins of her horse in his hand enabling her to dismount.

"Wicked tongue, Joshua?" Jackson asked, stepping up to his side.

Joshua wanted to punch him. "Back off, Jackson."

"What? I think it's cute. You have a wicked tongue, brother."

After he dismounted his horse, he got right in Jackson's face. "I said back off and shut your trap. There is a lady present."

"Lady? Not if she let you do what I think she did. She's probably not—"

Joshua pulled back his fist, punching Jackson in the mouth. "Take it back."

"Fuck you!" he yelled, charging his brother, taking them both to the ground in a cloud of dust.

"Stop it!" Candace shouted, trying to pull them apart only to be grabbed around the waist by Joey and pulled aside.

"Let them duke it out. You can't stop this. It's the way it is with brothers."

"You fucking idiot! Get off me!" Jackson pulled back, punching Joshua in the jaw hard enough to knock him backward.

"Enough!" James pulled Joshua by the arm. "Knock it off you two. This is ridiculous."

"He started it. He punched me first." Jackson dabbed at his nose trying to stop the flow of blood.

"He was saying Candace wasn't a lady. He doesn't even know her, and she's more of a lady than any bitch you've been with lately, Jackson."

"Wait a damned minute."

"Don't go there."

"I said enough, you two. Is this how you treat a woman, Joshua? Fighting in front of her?"

"I'm sorry. He just pissed me off. I was fighting for her honor."

Candace stepped in front of him, placing her hand on the front of his shirt. "And I appreciate it. Thank you for being gallant."

"You're a lady, and I won't have that asshole calling you anything but a lady. What happened between us is just that, between us." He touched his swelling lip with the tips of his fingers and winced at the pain shooting across his face. "Fucker."

"You want more of me, buddy? Come on. I'll beat the shit out of you."

"I don't fucking think so, asswipe. You couldn't punch your way out of a paper bag."

James held his arm, preventing the two of them from fighting more. "Take your girl and go on up to the house. Lunch will be ready soon. Jackson and Joey can take care of the animals."

"What did I do?" Jackson asked, holding his side where Joshua had punched him.

"We'll talk about your rude behavior after Joshua and his girl leave."

His girl. I kind of like that. "Come on, Candace."

The lunch bell clanged as he took her hand and walked her through the tack room. He wouldn't take the time to admire his own handy work in the room, but it was there. Rows and rows of his customized bridles, a couple of saddles he'd made and many more small pieces he'd forged out of the pieces of leather he'd worked on. He loved it, loved working with leather, getting the patterns just right with his tools, bringing out the beautiful design before putting the entire saddle together. These things made him happy.

As they approached the main lodge for lunch, he slipped his hand to the small of her back. "I'm sorry about that back there."

"I'm flattered you beat up your brother for me. I've never had a guy do something like that before. It's chivalrous. Makes me smile even though I'm upset that you got hit." She reached up to touch his face. "Thank you."

"It's nothin'."

"Sure it is. You've got a fat lip because of me."

He leaned in to kiss her lightly. "I'd do it again in a heartbeat." She smiled even though he winced at the pain in his lip. "Ouch."

"Poor baby."

"You can kiss me all over later to make me feel better." He stuck out his puffy lip in a little pout.

"I'll do that."

He smiled, and then frowned. *Damn lip hurts.* "Let's get some grub. I want to show you around the ranch more after lunch."

"Sounds good to me."

As they made their way inside toward the family table, his mother stopped him. "What happened to you?"

"I ran into Jackson's fist."

"Figures. Where are your brothers?"

"Dad is at the stable with Jackson and Joey."

His mother hobbled around on crutches now after her accident a few months prior. She'd been in physical therapy for a while, but she still couldn't walk on it, and plaster remained in place around her leg. "Damn thing."

"You shouldn't be up on it."

"I can't sit in a wheelchair the whole time." She put herself in a chair with a groan. "Joshua, would you get me some tea, please?"

"Sure, Mom." He poured some sweet tea into a glass before bringing it to her spot at the table. "Do you need me to get your plate?"

"No, Jeff is getting it, but thank you."

He glanced at the crowd in the dining room. It wasn't much since it was getting onto the downtime for the ranch. October always proved to be slower than September. They would all be heading out to Hawaii soon for Jeremiah and Callie's wedding. They had one of his uncles coming in to manage the place while they went. It would be fun. He'd never been to Hawaii before. They wouldn't stay long though. They were needed on the ranch. "Would you like to sit at the one of the empty tables or we can sit here at the family table."

"I don't want to take up someone's spot. Why don't we sit at the other table over there?"

"No problem." He led her to a table in the back and they took a seat. "You can go get your plate if you wish."

"Aren't you eating?"

"We have to wait until the guests are served. Mom's rules."

She patted the bench for him to sit beside her. "I'll wait then until you get yours. I'm sure there is plenty of food."

"Oh yeah. There always is," he replied straddling the bench seat in order to face her. "What other things do you want to experience while you're here?"

"Everything."

He laughed, regretting it immediately when his mouth started to throb again.

"I'm sorry. I didn't mean to make you laugh." She leaned in and kissed his fat lip. "There. It should feel better now."

"Of course. Kisses always make me feel better." He waggled his eyebrows at her, making her laugh in turn.

"Such a ham. Not the least bit modest, are you."

"Nope."

He glanced at the group and noticed his family getting up to get their food, so he directed her toward the line.

Jeff and Terri stood in front of them with Ben while Grandma kept an eye on James.

"When is the baby due?" Candace asked.

"Soon." Terri skimmed her hand down her abdomen. "I wish he or she would hurry up. I've been ready for a while now."

"You don't know what it is?"

"No. We wanted to be surprised," she said, leaning into Jeff's embrace.

"You two won't be going to Hawaii then, huh?" Joshua added.

"No. We'll stay here and help Uncle Nathan with the ranch. I wish we could be there, but Terri can't fly. It's too late in the pregnancy."

"It's better this way." Terri rubbed her lower back with her hand as she rested the other one on her abdomen.

"Are you okay, babe?" Jeff asked, worry making his eyebrows scrunch together.

"Yeah, just some back pain."

"You were cramping last night too. Don't you think we should go to the hospital?"

"Maybe, but it's too early. The baby isn't due for another two weeks."

"You went early with James too though."

"True."

"Let's go. Better now that you haven't had breakfast or lunch. You know they don't want you to eat anything."

"I'm not that hungry anyway." They stepped out of line. "See you later, Joshua."

"Take care, Terri. I hope it's time, for your sake."

"Me too. I'm really uncomfortable. He or she is going to be a big baby." She waved to both him and Candace while they moved toward the food.

After a minute or two of talking to Nina, they headed outside the doors of the main lodge in what he assumed to be a mad dash to the hospital in San Antonio. Joshua hoped things went okay for his brother and soon-to-be sister-in-law. He frowned as he twisted up his mouth. It was about time Jeff put a ring on that girl's finger.

"They seem like a great couple."

"It was hard going with them when they first met. Terri is an architect, and she was working with land developers to put in a housing project on some adjacent land. She found a rare bird on the property that stopped them doing anything with it. They weren't happy, but she saved us a major problem."

They moved forward a few steps, picking up empty plates to fill with food.

"They seem very much in love."

"It wasn't that way at first. Jeff hated her." He put a hamburger bun on his plate as he reached the meat and Mandy slid a patty onto his bun. "Well Jeff was married before. Ben is his with his first wife. It was a bad breakup, but he got custody of his son. We found out later his mother was doing drugs. She overdosed a few years ago."

"How sad."

"Yeah, but Terri more than makes up for the mother she wasn't. She's great with the kids."

"How many of your brothers are paired up now? There are nine of you, right?"

"Yes, nine of us. Five out of nine of us have significant others. Jeff and Terri are the only ones not married and I think he'll be taking care of that issue soon. At least I hope so, but he's really gun-shy."

"It sounds like he had a right to be."

They finished grabbing their food and headed back to the table they had secured before to eat. "You don't know the half of it." Joshua squirted some ketchup onto his hamburger and squished down the bun on top before he took a healthy bite. "His first wife cheated on their wedding night with the local sheriff."

Candace picked up a French fry, dipped it in the pool of ketchup she had on her plate before she popped it into her mouth. "Seriously?"

"Yep."

"What a bitch."

"We thought so. It was a special day when Jeff finally saw the light." He chuckled. "He's crazy about the girl he's with now."

"They have a couple kids, right?"

"This pregnancy is their second together and they have Ben. He's a great kid. Growing like a weed. He'll be tall like all the Youngs."

"You are tall."

"Six foot four and a half. I'm one of the tallest of us boys."

"Wow."

She took a healthy bite of her hamburger, leaving a small bit of ketchup on her lips. The swipe of her tongue across the surface had his cock rising to meet the occasion, and he hoped they'd be able to take care of his problem soon. Otherwise, he might just explode with merely a touch.

"How was it growing up with such a big family?"

"Fun and hard. We get along for the most part. Better now that we're all older and a little more mature." One of her eyebrows rose in a questioning quirk. "For the most part. Do you have a big family?"

"Not as big as yours." She took another bite of her hamburger before she went on, "I have two sisters and a brother."

"Where are you in the pecking order?"

"The baby."

"Ah, the spoiled one."

"No, I'm not!"

"Yeah, Joey doesn't think he is either, but he was always the favorite."

She released a sound that came across as a choking gurgle. It didn't sound very sexy at all, but it sure matched the frown on her face. "I'm not the favorite by a long shot. My brother is by far."

"I'm sure your siblings wouldn't agree."

"I don't know. I've never asked them."

He liked teasing her. "Should I call them and ask?" He pulled out his cell. "Give me the number and I'll…"

She swiped the phone from his hand. "No." A moment later, she started pushing buttons on the screen. "Shall we see how many female phone numbers you have in here?"

"I'll take that back now." He grabbed for the phone, but she kept it out of reach across the table.

"What, Joshua? You don't want me to know how many girlfriends you've had?"

"I have only had one girlfriend. I told you that."

"Well now. I see several female names here. Cindy. Trish. Melanie." She thumbed through more of his contact list. "Theresa. Sharon. Oh look! One with stars next to it. What does that mean, Joshua?"

"Nothing."

"Really? Why don't I believe you?"

He jumped to his feet, grabbing the phone out of her hand. "It's none of your business."

"Well now, why didn't you say so in the beginning?"

Her innocent little smile didn't fool him. Why did she want to know how many women he'd been with?

He would satisfy her needs. That's all she needed to know. "I'll take care of you when the time comes."

"I'm jealous. You don't have me in your contact list."

"I don't have your number."

"Well then. Let me give it to you." She held out her hand for his phone. When he handed it to her, she punched in her number into his contact list although she probably scrolled through the numbers too. "Now you have it."

She gave him a saucy wink and returned to eating her hamburger like nothing happened. When he slowly took his seat, he had wondered what she was up to. Did she only want a short term thing for the time she was here or did she have other plans in mind? Maybe she would find herself more attracted to one of his brothers?

Liking her was the easy part. He liked her a lot, but could he trust her? Probably not. She was all woman, and he found most of them lacking in the trust department.

Chapter Five

Candace held on tight when Joshua took them over several bumps in the road. Holding on to his waist or wrapping her arms around his middle did funny things to her insides, even though she tried to concentrate on keeping herself on the four-wheeler. They were already covered in mud from the helmets on their heads to the boots on their feet. Good thing she had a face mask on her helmet or she'd have mud in her teeth. A shower would be a priority before dinner.

Joshua pulled over to the side of the dirty road. "Do you want to drive? We can go back and get one of the other four-wheelers. That way you can have your own."

"No. I'm good. I like holding on to you."

"Do you want to make a trip through the mud again?" He removed his goggles for a moment, leaving the shape of them around his eyes.

Laughter bubbled in her chest. He looked hilarious with mud spattered on his clothes and face. "Sure. The mud sounds fun. Maybe tomorrow we can take two and I'll drive."

"Of course, although I like you sitting behind me." He wiped a bit of mud clinging to her neck. "You look cute all dressed in mud."

He slid back onto the four-wheeler in the front before she grabbed his waist to hold on. Mud sprayed in all different directions as he revved the engine and rushed the mud pit. Jonathan and Jackson did the same from the other direction, effectively spraying them with a large wave of brown. She was certain she would drown in all this watered down dirt.

She had to admit, seeing him interact with his brothers without fighting, was something she enjoyed. They had the camaraderie of a close family even though Jackson had fought with Joshua earlier. They seemed to have forgotten the argument as they gunned the machines back through the mud again. "You do this in your truck too?"

"Yeah. It's even more fun in the truck." Joshua unwrapped the tight Velcro around his wrist to check the time. "We need to get back. Dinner will be happening soon, and I'm sure you want to take a shower before you eat."

"Yes, I do. I have mud in places I didn't know mud could go."

"I can help you wash certain places." He waggled his eyebrows which was hilarious because they were caked in mud.

She giggled at the face he was making. "You are incorrigible, you know that?"

"Yep." Joshua signaled for his brothers to join him. "We're going back. It's almost supper time."

"Okay," Jonathan replied as Jackson nodded. "I need a shower anyway."

"Yeah, us too."

With Jackson in the front of the pack, Jonathan in the middle and Joshua in the rear, they headed back toward the lodge house.

Today had been one of the best days of her life. This cowboy thing was pretty cool. She liked the peaceful atmosphere of the ranch. She couldn't wait to experience more of Joshua's lifestyle. She wanted the

experience of living with such a large family. She
wanted to see a baby horse born. She liked getting up at
dawn to take in the rising sun over the mountains and
feeding the donkeys. She could almost get used to
living like this. There were no honking cars, no hustling
people from place to place like little ants trying to stay
ahead, and people out here didn't hurt each other. They
didn't shoot at each other over stupid things. Yeah, she
thought she might be getting attached to this way of
life.

They pulled the four-wheelers next to the
equipment barn to hose them off before putting them
away. She excused herself as Joshua started spraying
the four-wheeler they used, to take a shower and get
ready for dinner.

When she crested the second floor landing, she
smelled a flowery perfume right before she felt a sharp
sting, like something scratched her across the arm. She
glanced down to find three angry red welts across her
forearm. "What the hell?"

She shoved the key into the lock, quickly went
inside and shut the door. "That was weird."

After she calmed her stuttering heart, she strip off
her muddy clothes and tossed them into the bathroom
tub so they wouldn't get the whole room dirty. She
would wash them out before she took a shower.

She washed her hands and forearms in the sink
before she grabbed some clean underwear from her
suitcase to take a shower. She managed to get most of
the mud washed out of the clothes before she put them
in the sink. "I think they have a washer I can use."

Hot water sprayed from the overhead rain
showerhead, soaking her hair and washing more mud
down the drain. She hoped all the dirt didn't clog the

tub. She should have had Joshua spray her off before she came upstairs. *Oh well. Too late now.*

Minutes later, with her shower completed, she grabbed a big fluffy towel off the rack, tied her hair up in one, and then draped another around her body. She glanced down at the marks on her arm wondering where they came from. She hadn't bumped into the doorframe or anything like that. *Huh.* She shrugged as she stepped back into the bedroom part of her room to get some clean clothes. A tank top and a pair of jeans should do. She had slip on sandals she could wear since her boots were now covered in mud.

She couldn't help but smile. Four-wheeling had been so much fun, she knew they would have to do it again before her time on the ranch concluded. And mudding with the trucks. She had to experience that too. Everything cowboy sounded like a hell of a lot of fun.

As she slipped on her clothes, she heard the dinner bell ring from outside. She'd heard what she assumed was Joshua coming up the stairs right before she went into the shower. What would it be like making love with him under the hot spray of the water? The vision of him standing in all his glory at the pond came back in a rush, making her wish they could just lock themselves away for the night. She could slowly lick every inch of his body, from the top to the bottom without missing an inch.

With a long drawn out sigh, she finished slipping on her sandals in order to go downstairs for supper. They ate a lot of food here, she would probably gain twenty pounds before she went home. *Ah well, a little more time at the gym wouldn't hurt anyway.* She wasn't skinny by any means, but she did have a nice curvy figure, and she wanted to make sure she kept the love handles at bay.

When she opened the door, she almost ran smack dab into Joshua. "Wow, you're quick."

"I didn't take a long one. Just washed the mud off." He did a slow glance from her hair to her feet. "You look refreshed."

"I feel it too. I probably washed a ton of mud down the drain between washing out my clothes and taking a shower."

"It's fine. We do it all the time. Mom and Dad have it down pat on the dirt part. We have a muddin' party about once a month anyway until it gets too cool."

"Good. I won't feel guilty about the pound of dirt then." She wrapped her hand and forearm into the crook of his elbow.

"What happened to your arm?"

"I'm not sure. I didn't notice it before I came upstairs, but I must have caught it on a branch while we were out on the four-wheelers. It started to sting when I reached my door." She turned her arm so she could see it better. It looked like fingernail marks. "Weird, huh?"

"Yeah. Just be careful. We don't want you hurt while you're here."

"Oh, I will."

They headed downstairs to eat, making small talk as they walked. "What's for dinner?"

"It's steak night. They grill New York strip steaks once a week."

"Yum. I love steak."

Once they made it to the bottom of the stairs, she noticed the family already serving themselves. They wandered over to get in line. "We can eat at another table or sit with the family?"

"Have you heard anything on Jeff and Terri?"

"She's in labor and they expect the new baby soon. Mom and Dad are at the hospital already. There are plenty of seats left at the family table."

"Sure. Let's do that." After they filled their plates of food, he asked her what she wanted to drink as they made their way to the family table. "Tea is fine. No, make that lemonade."

"Great. If you take my plate, I'll get the drinks."

She took his plate from his hand and headed to the table, trying to decide where to sit. The family had grown so large with the additions of women for the guys and their children, there were two family tables these days.

"You can sit here, Candace." Jonathan offered the two chairs next to his that were empty.

"I don't want to take anyone's seat."

"You aren't. This is where Jeff and Terri usually sit. Since they aren't here, they're free."

"Great!" She took the seat next to Jonathan, sitting Joshua's plate next to hers. "I would love to sit and talk websites with you. I've looked at the ranch site, and I could make some suggestions, if you don't mind."

"Do you do website design?"

"Some. I'm a programmer, but I do some designing on the site as well. There are a couple of things I could help you with."

"That would be awesome. I haven't been formally trained. I learned everything on my own."

"Really? That's fabulous! I went through four years of college to learn web design and programming. I'm returning in the fall for my master's degree." She glanced back at Joshua, noting the frown on his face. "Something wrong?"

"No."

He looked down at where she placed her hand on Jonathan's arm. Okay, obviously he doesn't like her touching his brother. *Hmm.* "Sorry. I'm a touchy feely kind of person."

"You can touch me all you want." Joshua shoved a forkful of potato salad into his mouth.

"Just don't touch your brothers?"

"You're mine."

"I am?"

"For now anyway."

"I'm not a cheater, Joshua. If you want exclusive while I'm here, I'm good with that."

The tension in his shoulder eased as the frown pulling his eyebrows down did too. Jealousy. Interesting concept. He didn't like her being too friendly with his brothers. Apparently, he'd been cheated on at one point too. Maybe the one love of his life had not only chosen someone else over him, but cheated too?

"I can do exclusive."

"Good. I'm all for that. I want you all to myself anyway." Jonathan snorted and rolled his eyes. "Someday you'll be there too, Jonathan, so be quiet over there."

"I'm not looking for a girlfriend."

"That's usually when you find her."

The rest of the meal she listened to the conversations around the table. Some speculation went on about whether Jeff and Terri would have a girl or a boy, then discussion about some work around the ranch came up. The women broke off at some point to talk amongst themselves. It appeared Paige and Peyton were pretty good friends while Callie chatted with Mesa about things going on in town. The boys did their own huddles, bantering about one thing or another. *Wouldn't it be great to be a part of this family?* Whoa!

She shook her head. *Nope. Not going there.*

"Are you okay?"

"Yeah, just thinking."

"About?"

"Getting you between the sheets."

"How about shooting a game of pool?" he asked, steering the conversation back to safer ground around his family, she guessed.

She'd noticed a pool table in the main part of the lodge when she checked in, but tonight she wasn't into playing pool. She wanted hot, kinky, sweaty sex. "Nah. We could take a swim though."

"The pool isn't heated."

"I could use a cool down because," she leaned in close to his ear, "I'm really horny."

"Me too." He glanced at her half eaten plate. "Are you finished?"

"Nope. I'm going to eat this entire steak." She giggled, skimming her hand over his erection. "You'll have to suffer for a little longer." She cut another small piece off her steak and stuck it into her mouth, humming her appreciation for the taste of the meat. Making him suffer a little in his state of arousal seemed kind of mean, but then again, she had to suffer too. Her pussy throbbed with each beat of her heart, reminding her of the need he made her feel just being around him, never mind his kisses.

Conversation swirled around them as she picked at the rest of the food on her plate. The meal was fantastic, the meat cooked to perfection, the potatoes were smooth and fluffy and the vegetables were crisp. Every

meal at the ranch reminded her of cookouts at home
with her family, and she was sure that's the persona
they were going for with the ranch. It fit.

* * * *

Joshua watched Candace take another bite of her
food and chew. *God, she has sexy lips.* The way she
wrapped them around the tines of her fork made him
want to jerk her from her chair and haul her ass up the
stairs to his room. If he had to wait one more minute, he
might die because his balls were about to explode.

"Aren't you hungry?" she asked, her eyes
twinkling with mirth.

She knew exactly what she was doing to him. "I
find myself wanting something else to eat."

"Oh? Dessert looks great too. I could get you some
if you'd like."

"I want another kind of dessert."

"Really? Like what?"

He leaned in and pressed his lips to her ear.
"Pussy." She choked a little on her last bite of food as
he let the warmth of his breath caress the side of her
neck. "I'm going to lick you all over from the tips of
your gorgeous breasts to your clit. I know how much
you enjoy my tongue."

She shivered under the touch of his tongue along
her neck.

"All right, you two. Enough with the hands on at
the dinner table. You know Mom would have a fit to
see you acting this way, Joshua," Jeremiah scolded as
he draped an arm around Callie's shoulders.

"When is the wedding?" Candace sounded breathless as a sigh escaped her lips. "I heard you were all flying to Hawaii?"

"Yes," Callie answered. "We want to get married on the beach with just our families around. Very small, private ceremony."

"Awesome. Sounds like a really romantic little interlude."

"Have you been to Hawaii?" Callie asked, pushing her plate away.

"Yes, several times actually. Living in California, it's not too expensive to go."

"I lived in California before Joel and I got together," Mesa added. "Where do you live?"

"Anaheim."

"Very nice. I lived outside of Pasadena before I moved out here."

"Do you like it here?"

"I love it. It's quiet. I can write and soak up the cowboy atmosphere all I want."

"You're a writer?"

"Yes. I write romance novels, contemporary western romance novels."

"Oh cool. I read a lot. I could never write. You must be very talented."

Joel laughed as he tugged on a curl hanging from the back of the bun on Mesa's head. "She's sells more now than ever. I wouldn't have to work if I didn't want to. She got a sizable advance from her publisher with her last book."

"What's the titles to a couple? I might have read you."

"I write under Mesa West."

Excitement lit up her face. Apparently, Candace was a big fan of Mesa's books although he didn't see the big hullabaloo where Mesa was concerned.

"Oh wow! I love your cowboy romances. I've read everything you put out. This is awesome! I've never met a real live author before."

Mesa blushed. "Thank you. I love talking to my fans."

Candace bounced a little in the chair. "I'm thrilled!" She frowned. "I wish I had some of my paperbacks with me. I would have you sign them." Everyone at the table was smiling as she gushed over Mesa. "You don't understand. She's Mesa West."

"Yeah, we know." Joel laughed before he reached over and kissed her on the cheek. Their infant daughter began to fuss. Mesa stood and excused herself from the table.

"Your baby is as cute as a button."

"She takes after her momma," Joel gushed a little watching Mesa take the baby from her chair before she went around the corner to take care of her.

"What's her name?"

"Elizabeth Marie after my grandmother and Mesa's mother."

"What a beautiful name."

"We thought so."

"Is she a good baby? I don't think I've heard her cry much."

"Oh yeah. She's already sleeping well into the night. She only gets up once for a feeding."

"How precious."

"Thank you."

"How many grandkids are there now?"

"Jeff and Terri are on their third. Mesa and I have one and Paige and Jacob have boy girl twins."

"Twins? Holy moly."

"Yeah, it keeps us busy," Jacob added, nodding to the two in high chairs in the corner.

She swiveled around to look at the twins. She really had very expressive eyes.

"How cute they are. I bet they are a handful. What are they, about a year?"

Jacob and Paige beamed with pride. "Fourteen months. They're walking and getting into everything."

"I bet."

"Do you want kids?"

"Someday. I have three siblings, but it's not near as crazy busy as having nine kids like your family."

"We hope to have a big family too," Paige answered, glancing at her daughter while she fed herself fingers foods. "We want six at least."

"We do?" Jacob added with a bit of a frown.

"Yes we do. We discussed this, Jacob."

Jacob laughed as he slipped his arm around his wife. "Call me when these two are out of diapers, and we'll discuss having more." Paige leaned over and kissed him soundly on the mouth. "Practice makes perfect."

"I love practicing with you."

"I know you do."

"When are you planning to settle down?" Jacob focused his gaze on Joshua's face.

He cocked an eyebrow, shooting his brother a butt out look. "Someday. I'm not in a hurry."

Jacob glanced her way, giving her the once over before he glanced back his way.

Candace held up her hands. "Don't look at me. I don't even live here. I'm just hanging out for a few weeks, soaking up the cowboy thing."

"I see."

"Good. Matchmaking needs to be out of the picture here."

"Stay away from our mother then. She loves hooking us up with a girl she thinks is perfect for us. Right, honey?" Jacob asked Paige.

"Oh yeah. She's great for meddling." Paige smiled. "I love her to death, but she loves matchmaking."

"I'll avoid her like the plague then."

They laughed in unison making him wonder if they didn't have plans already in the works. He hoped they stayed out of his business, but he had to be careful. His mother loved to get in the middle of relationships. She'd done it with all his brothers. He frowned. Maybe she had something there. After a moment, he glanced at Candace. She would do, although like she said, she didn't live here. He shrugged. She'd be good for a few weeks of some fun, but he should probably look closer to home if he wanted to find the woman he could maybe spend his life with. Long distance relationships didn't work very well.

His thoughts drifted to the past, to Loren. He'd been in love with her a few years ago. In love enough to want to marry her, but she'd been offered a job in New York with a prestigious advertising firm. She'd packed up her stuff and left without so much as a long goodbye. His heart hadn't been the same since. Giving it to someone else didn't seem possible, but he could find someone compatible to spend his life with. Didn't mean his heart had to get involved though.

The conversation moved onto other things besides his lack of relationship status, for which he was mighty thankful. He didn't need his brothers or his mother focusing on him. When the time was right, he'd find someone to settle down with. It didn't mean it had to be now.

Joshua watched Candace while she continued to eat. He wanted to feel the long, silky strands of her hair through his fingers. Right now, she hand it pulled back in a low ponytail to keep it off her neck, he figured, but he really wanted to have it around her shoulders while she rode him into next week.

His cock stiffened painfully behind the fly of his jeans. Yeah, he wanted her, needed her with every breath in his body. He hoped they'd get to that part tonight after the bonfire he planned to take her to. Sex with her would be totally worth the wait. After he cleared his throat and shifted on the chair to try to relieve some of the pressure, he finished his food by shoveling the last few bites into his mouth. "What do you want to do after dinner?"

"I'm not sure."

"I should probably do a little work in the barn, oiling up the leather. You can either help me with that or you can brush down the horses if you like."

"Sounds like a plan."

They both stood, grabbed their plates and headed for the dirty dish bin.

"Hey, Joshua."

"Oh hey, Mandy."

"Are we still on for later?"

"Later?" he asked, confusion rushing through him. Had he made a date with Mandy he'd forgotten? Not that he was interested in her that way, but he didn't want to disappoint a friend.

"You know? You were going to show me how to braid the leather for something for my mom for her birthday coming up."

"Oh that. Yeah, I can show you. I'll be out in the stable oiling up the bridles and saddles. Come and find me."

"Okay." She smiled, a bright spread her lips in a wide arch, smile.

She really was a nice girl and kind of pretty too, although he knew she had the hots for one of the unattached brothers, not him.

"I'll catch you after we get the dinner dishes done."

Candace stepped up and held out her hand. "Hi. I'm Candace. One of the guests for now. I just wanted to say the food is delicious."

"I'll pass it onto the cook. She'll be pleased. I'm glad you like it."

"Definitely, especially the desserts. They are to die for."

"I know what you mean. The chocolate mousse is fabulous. I think I've gained twenty pounds since I started working here from eating the desserts. It all went straight to my butt."

"No way. You look great."

"Well, thank you." Mandy cocked her head and looked at him. "You need to keep her around. She's good for my ego, Joshua."

"Mine too. She kind of likes me."

"I'm sure you'd be a fabulous catch."

He puffed out his chest as he adjusted the hat on his head. "Of course I would." The two women laughed when he smiled. "Let's head out to the barn, Candace, and I'll show you were everything is."

With his hand at the small of her back, he guided her out the door of the lodge, toward the stables and barn. He loved the smell of leather, horses, hay, and everything in the big red structure. It always seemed to calm him when he would get upset as a child. Working with leather pieces gave him peace from the stresses of growing up in such a big family.

"What are you working on now?"

"A custom saddle for my dad for his birthday."

"Wow. Can I see it?"

"Sure. It's been a bitch to keep it hidden from him, but it'll be worth it in the end. I think he's going to love it." He opened the small workshop door on the right side of the barn where he kept his supplies. It had taken several months of hand working the leather to get it just right. It was almost finished. The chocolate colored carved leather gleamed in the light of the room.

"Oh my." Her hand slipped over the carvings of the horses in the leather. "You did this?"

"Yep."

"This is magnificent, Joshua. You're really good."

"Thanks."

"I can't imagine how long this must have taken you to carve."

"Not too long, but it was very precise. I couldn't mess up at all."

"It's beautiful." Her voice came out in a whisper of awe.

The pleasure on her face made him feel like a million bucks. He'd never had anyone exclaim over his work before like she was.

She turned back toward him to put her hand on his chest as she stepped closer. "Would you make me something to remember you by?"

"Like what?"

"How about a cowgirl belt? I could get one of those silver belt buckles to remind me of my time here on the ranch." She frowned a little as she stepped back. "I don't want you to take away from getting your dad's present done though."

He got closer, wanting to feel her hand on his chest again. He liked her hands on him, touching, exploring. The thoughts drove him a little crazy since they hadn't had a chance to do anything related to actual sex except the little oral he'd given her at the pond. With a sigh of expectation, he said, "A belt wouldn't take long at all."

"I would love that."

Her breath flittered across his lips, making them tingle in anticipation. "I'm going to kiss you."

"I wish you would."

With her back pressed against the wood siding, he leaned in and pressed his lips against hers. She felt wonderful, all soft like a fluffy blanket. Closing his eyes, he relished the feel of her lips against his own. She groaned and leaned into his body, wrapping her arms around his neck as she pressed her breasts into his chest. His hands settled on her hips before sliding around her back to bring her closer still. He wouldn't want to fuck her in his office, but man did he want her.

He lifted her, planting her butt on the edge of his desk, pushing the carving tools and template off to the back.

"I want you, Joshua." She trailed kiss across his chin and down his neck, stopping at the opening of his shirt while she began working the buttons loose.

"I want you too. I need to feel your heat around me, but I don't want to do this here."

Her lips blazed a trail down the center of his chest while she got each shirt button undone. Her hands scalded him as she parted the material, pulling the tails from his jeans.

"Do you have a condom?"

"Yeah, in my wallet in my pants."

"Lock the door."

"Are you sure?"

She tossed her shirt to the side after she pulled it over her head, leaving her in nothing but her frilly, pink bra. He wondered if her underwear matched as he stepped back to lock the door.

"Hell yeah. What a better place than surrounded by the smell of leather. It turns me on."

God, she's gorgeous.

She reached behind her back to unhook her bra, when he turned to secure the door. The last thing he wanted was one of his brothers to walk in on this.

Her breasts were perfect, nicely rounded with pert little nipples begging for the touch of his tongue.

She leaned back on her elbows, thrusting her breasts in his direction as she begged with her eyes and her lips. "Lick them."

With his hands on either side of her hips, braced against the metal desk top, he leaned in and took the left nipple between his lips. It was either his imagination running wild or something, but he thought for sure it tasted like a ripe little berry on his tongue.

She grabbed his hat from his head and tossed it on top of the file cabinet in the corner before she speared her fingers through his hair. He loved having her fingers threaded through his hair, cradling his head against her chest.

"Mmmm."

A low purr escaped her mouth, making him smile against her breast. He switched to the other breast to give it some attention while he palmed the left one, rolling the nipple between his thumb and finger. She had beautiful breasts. Just right to fit in his hand.

She worked the belt buckle at his waist until it was loose and hanging front his pants. "I need to touch you."

"Go ahead," he said, jerking the shirt from his shoulders while she unbuttoned and unzipped the catch on his jeans.

When her warm hand found his cock through his boxers, he hissed low in his throat at the shock her touch caused.

"You're a pretty big guy."

"Not really."

"Bigger than anyone I've had before."

"Is that going to be a problem?"

"I don't think so. I can't wait to feel all of this inside me."

He unfastened her jeans before grabbing them at the waist to work them off her hips. When he had them down around her ankles, he pushed them all the way off leaving her totally naked on his desk with her legs spread, ready for his touch.

His desk chair sat nearby. He grabbed it and sat down. He wanted to be at the right angle to pleasure her before he fucked her silly. The plan was to keep her on the brink until she begged him to fuck her hard.

He grabbed her hips and pulled her close. She braced her heels on the edge of the desk.

When he buried his face between her gorgeous thighs, he heard her sigh. Her pussy lips glistened with his saliva and her juices as he licked, sucked, and worshipped her flesh with his tongue. He slipped two fingers into her pussy, feeling the grip of her excitement on his digits. She was amazingly responsive to his touch. He wanted it to go on and on.

"Joshua, please, make me come."

"I'd love to." He sucked her clit into his mouth, rubbing first one side, and then the other. She squirmed on the desk top trying to get closer.

The little whimpers and mewls escaping from her mouth drove him crazy.

"Oh God." She exhaled on a rush. Her pussy gripped him in a vice-like hold when she came apart on a cry of ecstasy. "Joshua."

His name on her lips had him as hard as a brick, ready for the scalding heat of her pussy to envelope his flesh in her tight grip.

He wiped his face with the back of his hand, grinning like a damned fool. "Better?"

"For now." She reached out to take hold of his cock. "I want this now."

Swiping his wallet from the back pocket of his jeans, he groaned as she palmed him. "Easy, darlin'. It's loaded."

"I'm glad."

He pushed his jeans to the floor, taking his boxers along with them until he stood in front of her, bare and raring to go. After he quickly rolled the latex condom over his cock, his positioned it at her opening and slowly penetrated her.

A low moan escaped her lips as she closed her eyes and leaned back on her hands. "Oh my God. That's perfect."

When he was fully inside her, he stopped his movements to catch his breath. If he didn't slow this down, he would come way before he was ready to. He wanted to savor this first moment with her, feel every ripple of her sweet cunt around his dick, and remember this time for the rest of his life. She was one hot babe, hot enough to burn through the wall around his heart if he wasn't careful.

"Move please. I'm dying here."

He eased himself in and out, very slowly while she tossed her head from side to side, balling her hands into fists on the desk top.

"You're killing me."

"I want this to last. I'm so primed, I'll blow too fast."

"Don't worry, we can do it again later. For now, fuck me hard, Joshua. Please!"

Bracketing her hips with his hands, he began to fuck her in earnest, shoving his aching flesh into her hot core fast enough he banged the desk against the wall, rattling the bridles and leather he had hanging there.

"Yes, yes, yes!"

He captured her lips in a devastating kiss when he felt his balls draw up tight against his groin. If he didn't bring her along, he would hate himself in the end. He snaked his hand between them, grabbing her clit in a sharp pinch as he continued to pound into her.

She exploded on a high cry of ecstasy while he lost his control of his own climax, shooting his load into the latex reservoir.

As they slowly came down from their volatile climax, he cradled her head against his chest, loving the feel of her warm breath on his skin.

"That was…"

"I know."

"You okay?"

"I'm fabulous."

He slowly withdrew from her while they both groaned from the lack of intimacy. He loved being inside her, around her, feeling her gripping his cock like a vice.

She was one hot number, and he planned to use her well in the time she was with him.

Yep, he had plans all right, if he could just keep his head on straight in the process.

Chapter Six

The glow she felt from her evening with Joshua wouldn't leave her as she sat staring into the bonfire's light. He sure rocked her world with his love making in his office, and she wasn't quite sure what to make of it.

With her hand in his, they sat listening to the conversations of the other guests around the fire while the kids roasted marshmallows. She'd always loved S'mores when she was a kid, and she wondered if there was one she could convince to let her borrow their stick.

"Here." Joshua handed her a long piece of metal with a fork at the end.

"How did you know?"

"You were eyeing the S'mores the kids were eating, so I figured you wanted one. There are supplies on the table over there. It's something we always have when we do bonfires for the guests. It wouldn't be a campfire without S'mores."

She giggled while he stuck two marshmallows on the end of her roaster. "You roast those nice and melty, and I'll get the chocolate and graham crackers."

He wandered to the table being manned by his mother to retrieve the makings of their S'mores, while she admired the cut of his jeans across his butt and the way his shirt molded to his shoulders. *Damn, the man is built like nothing I've ever seen.* He reminded her of the romance novels Mesa wrote, thinking she might have shaped some of her cowboys after the sexy inspiration she had on the ranch. Why the hell not? She definitely had the goods to back up her fantasies here.

Candace watched as he smiled and exchanged a few words with his mother. They seemed like such a close family, it reminded her of her family back in California. Her dad worked a lot and her mother was a stay at home mom who did everything with the kids when they were growing up. She wished her dad had spent a little more time with them when they were children, but he loved them. This she knew, and she also knew he worked so much because he wanted them to have things he didn't have as a child.

He'd grown up very poor, with an absentee father and without much of a home life. He'd made his first million by the time he'd turned twenty-five, investing in computers when they first got to be the *in* thing. Yes, she and siblings had grown up with money, but they had to work for anything special, doing paper routes or working at the local fast food place. Her mom and dad agreed on teaching their kids the morals of a hard day's work, even with the trust fund left to her mother by her granddaddy.

As Joshua came back toward her, he smiled with a little tilt of his lips meant only for her. Her toes curled when she remembered those lips on hers, his tongue on her most private places, and how he'd brought her to such delight, she'd cried out in her ecstasy.

"You look like the cat who ate the canary," Mandy said, sitting down on the bench next to her.

"Who me?"

"Yeah."

Joshua sat on her other side, holding the chocolate and graham crackers until the marshmallows were done. She'd been admiring him too much to roast them until he returned.

"Why would you say that?"

"Oh, I don't know."

She grinned a little Cheshire cat spread of the lips, making Candace wonder exactly what she's was up to.

"I came by the office, Joshua, but I think you were a little busy."

"Huh?"

"You know, so you could show me how to braid that leather, but when I went to knock, some awfully strange sounds were coming from your office. I figured I'd wait until tomorrow."

"Oh shit." Candace felt her face flush hot. Mandy must have heard them having sex in his office.

"Sorry. I forgot you were coming by."

"No problem. I didn't want to disturb you."

"I'm sorry." Candace turned to apologize to Mandy, losing the marshmallows is the process from the end of the stick. "Crap."

"It's okay. There are more."

"But," she leaned toward him whispering, "she heard us."

"So?"

"But…"

"It's okay." He leaned in and kissed her on the lips. "No one else heard anything."

"I did!" Joey raised his hand from across the fire.

Her face turned red again.

"Me too." Jackson waved from their left. "Way to go, Joshua!"

Jeff raised his hand, as well as Jeremiah, Joel, and Jacob.

"Shit." She wanted to hide. "I'm so embarrassed.

"That's enough, boys. The poor girl is terrified now, I'm sure, and I know damned well most of you didn't hear anything because you were in the house with me," their mother answered, giving Candace a reprieve to believe the majority of them were giving her shit.

"Thank you."

"You're welcome and believe me, sweetie, around here, if the whole place hasn't heard one or another of these boys and their women, I would be surprised. Our barn gets a workout most of the time. With several of them paired off, sometimes they are hard pressed for alone time other than at their own homes. These are randy men. It comes with the territory of being a Texan."

Somehow that didn't make Candace feel all that much better. She couldn't look any of them in the face knowing they might have heard her and Joshua in the barn even though, as his mother said, they'd all been caught at one time or another. That brought her thoughts around to how many other women he'd brought out to the ranch and made love with. She really didn't want to know. He certainly knew his way around a woman's body. Experience wasn't in short supply where he was concerned.

"Well, we know Joshua is no virgin."

Jackson snorted a few feet away, but she wasn't sure who actually said the remark.

"None of you were virgins much past your thirtieth birthday, I don't believe," their mother replied.

"Mom!"

"Well you weren't and if you thought your father and I didn't know, you are in for a shock."

Candace glanced around, thankful to see the regular guests had all taken their leave sometime before. She hoped it was long before this conversation had begun.

The S'mores lay forgotten when the boys started bantering back and forth about their love lives as their wives and girlfriends just shook their heads at the chaos.

She really didn't know if this was normal behavior for the men, but it sure seemed to be as the women around the fire began having their own conversations that had nothing to do with the men or their conquests.

Mesa walked over, took her hand and drew her to their little corner of the campfire. "Come on. You can sit with us. They'll be at this a while. Trust me." Mesa's little girl slept soundly in her carrier at the women's feet. Little tuffs of dark hair graced the baby's head. Little chubby cheeks moved slightly while the baby sucked in her sleep, her little mouth moving ever so slightly.

"She's such a little doll."

"Thank you." Mesa smoothed her hand over the baby's head. "She's a good baby."

Jacob and Paige's twins played in a portable playpen nearby, with a couple of stuffed animals.

Terri was still in the hospital with the newest addition to the Young household, a little baby girl.

Candace was kind of surprised Jeff was at the bonfire when his woman was still in the hospital, but their mother mentioned earlier that Terri had chased him out so she could get some sleep before the baby and she came home to the rambunctiousness of two boys. Jeff had spread the pictures on his phone around to everyone already though and after Grandma and

Grandpa showed their pictures, they proclaimed her to be a beautiful little girl with her daddy's eyes.

"Are you okay, Candace?" Paige asked.

"Yeah, I'm fine. I'm just not used to all this. I don't have this big of a family and it's not all boys."

"You'll get used to it the longer you stick around."

"Well, I'm only here for a few weeks."

"Yeah, that's what a couple of us said too," Mesa added with a wicked little smile.

"No, really. I can't stay. I have a business to run."

"Uh-huh. I'll warn you now, once one of these boys gets you wrapped around their finger, it's impossible to let go. I know. I tried," Peyton said, licking marshmallow off her fingers after she stuffed the last of a S'more in her mouth.

"But you all are in love with your brother, I'm not in love with Joshua."

"Give it time."

Nina grinned from the fringes of their conversation, making Candace feel like she was in so much trouble, she should run back to Los Angeles right now. But when she glanced over at Joshua, she realized she didn't want to run anywhere, at least not for a bit yet. She still had some cowboying stuff to do and it included a lot more raunchy sex with a certain cowboy.

* * * *

Joshua walked her to her door on the second floor of the main lodge with an arm around her waist. He didn't want to say goodnight to her quite yet, so he stalled a bit when she leaned against the wall by putting his hands on either side of her head and leaning in. "Sorry about all the talk at the bonfire."

"It's okay. The girls kept me busy while you boys were doing your thing."

He grinned. "It's just the way we are around each other. The girls have kind of gotten used to it, I guess. They just let us be."

She fingered the button on his shirt. "Yeah, I got that much."

"Would you like to watch some television? It's still kind of early to turn in."

"What are we going to do tomorrow?"

"I figured we go ride fences again for a while. One of the horses went into labor tonight so you might want to see that if the foal comes."

"Oh, that would be fabulous! Do they come fast or slow? Can I touch the momma? What's it like?"

He laughed. "Whoa. Slow down, darlin'. You can watch, but not touch. The mare won't like it too much if there are lots of people involved."

"Okay." She bounced on her toes. "If she gets close tonight, can you wake me? I want to see this."

"I'll have my dad wake me, and then I'll come get you. Okay?"

"Deal." She clapped her hands in excitement. "This is going to be totally awesome!"

"You might not think so if it's at three in the morning."

"Oh, I will. I can sleep in tomorrow if nothing else."

"All right. It's a deal."

She glanced up through her lashes with a sneaky little grin on her lips, the same lips he's been dreaming about since they'd parted this afternoon.

"What do you want to watch on television?"

"I don't know. We have lots of movies in the main lodge. We can go down there, pop some popcorn, watch a chick flick and cuddle on the couch."

"Oh, I like the way you think, cowboy."

"Good." He looked down her body, and then back up. "Do you want to change into something a little more comfortable? If you have pajama pants or something, it would be a little better than stiff jeans."

"You just want me out of my clothes."

"Well that too, but I figured we could make love again after everyone is asleep for the night."

"Who all uses the main lodge for their bedroom?"

"My parents mostly, although Jonathan is the only other one with a room in the main lodge. Joey has a bunkroom in the stable, Jackson has one of the cabins out in the yard and all the guys already paired up have their own places except for Jeremiah and Callie. They're having their place built while they're getting married and on their honeymoon."

"Aren't you going to Hawaii too?"

"Yes, but it's not for another month."

"I'll be gone back to California then." She frowned, smoothing her hand over his chest, but didn't meet his eyes.

He wondered what she was thinking when she looked back up and smiled a sad little smile. Would she miss him just a little? He kind of hoped she would because he sure would miss her smile, her touch, her laugh, and everything else about her. He'd kind of grown fond of her in the few days she'd been with him. How would he feel when her time was over?

It wouldn't matter. He needed to get anything permanent out of his head right now. She lived in California. That was almost as far as New York where

Loren took off to, and he sure didn't want to go through that again. No siree. Not in this lifetime.

"What's the frown for?"

"Huh? Oh nothing. I was just thinking about how we have all this time left to get you your cowboy experience."

"It'll be gone before you know it."

"Yeah, probably, but you'll have the experience of a lifetime."

"True and I can't wait to experience more of this life. It's kind of growing on me."

"It is?"

"Yeah, the simplicity of it, the laid back way of life just makes me want to embrace it all the more."

He sighed, tucking a loose curl behind her ear. "I'll meet you downstairs in fifteen minutes. I'd like to take a shower."

"You sure you don't want me to join you? I kinda like shower sex."

She ran her tongue up his neck to his lips, flicking it against the edge in a torturous, tantalizing movement meant to drive him crazy. "Hmm. Maybe tomorrow. I'd like our next go round to be in a bed."

"Party pooper." She pouted a little bit before she turned toward the door and slipped her key into the lock.

As she pushed the door open, he felt fingers along his arm. The ghost was making her displeasure known when he felt a scratch and noticed a red welt coming up on his right forearm.

"What the hell?" Candace touched his arm where the welt had turned a bright red.

"It's nothing."

"Nothing? That's an angry looking scratch. Is there a loose piece on the doorframe or something?"

"No."

"Where did you scratch your arm? I didn't see it before."

He blew out a ragged breath as he felt fingers on his neck, brushing them off absently with his hand. "It's one of the ghosts. There is a female who has attached herself to me."

Her eyes widened as her mouth opened and closed a couple of time. "What?"

"Yeah. I feel her fingertips a lot especially out here in the hall."

"Is she here now?"

"Yes."

"You can feel her?"

"Yeah." He inhaled, taking in the sweet smell he was very familiar with. "Can you smell the perfume?"

"Yes."

"That's her. It's always the same smell and touch." He turned around and looked down the hall. "You need to leave me alone now. I'm here with Candace, so stop this nonsense." The perfume smell faded away on the breeze they felt from the window at the end of the hall, left open slightly to the night breeze.

"That's weird. It's gone now."

"Yep. She'll be back though, probably tomorrow."

"Is this a daily occurrence?"

"Every day."

"Wow," she whispered backing through her doorway and rubbing her arms. "That's kind of creepy. Does your family know about this?"

"A few of them. I don't talk about it much. She doesn't seem to bug anyone, but me so I just deal with it." Candace bit her lip, her eyes wide and nervous. "She won't hurt you."

"Sorry." She ran her hands up and down her forearms. "It makes me nervous is all."

"Do you want to sleep with me?"

"Can I?"

"Sure." He pushed her back into her room. "Go ahead and change. I'll meet you downstairs in a few, and we'll watch a movie." He smiled before running his fingertips down her cheek. "I won't even make it a scary one. We can watch some chick flick."

"That would be good."

"Okay. See you down there."

She backed into her room, slowly closing the door as she peeked out through the slit until the door clicked with the latch.

He shook his head. This ghost might be a problem if she got physical with him over his being with Candace. He might have to talk to his mother about it and see what they could do to bring in a medium or something. They needed to nip this in the bud. It hadn't bothered him before, but he wouldn't let the entity harm Candace.

After a moment, he headed down the hallway toward his own bedroom to take a shower. He smelled like horses, leather, hay and fire from being out near the bonfire tonight. He smiled. He kind of liked how embarrassed Candace got when his brother said he'd heard them, not that he really believed him because that's just how they rolled. They loved to harass each other over women, sex, trucks, and everything cowboy. The women in their lives had to get used to it, and he was glad Mesa, Paige, Peyton, Mandy, and Callinda had taken her under their wings and let her into their little circle of friends. It made him feel better about her being near his family.

What would it be like having her here all the time?

Whoa! Where the hell did that thought come from. No permanent things here. Nope. Not going to happen. Yeah, he wanted a wife someday, and Candace kind of fit the bill, but he couldn't think of her like that since she would be leaving soon.

Oh well.

He pushed open the door on his room, and then shut it behind him. A shower would feel good to wash away the grime and smells of the day so he could cuddle with one gorgeous woman for a few hours while they watched a movie, and then maybe he could get his dick wet before they slept for the night.

A cowboy could dream, couldn't he?

Chapter Seven

Candace felt a chill run down her spine. She wasn't sure why, but the whole ghost thing gave her the willies. To think it could affect its surroundings made her a little creeped out with everything.

After she grabbed her soft pajama pants, she stripped off her boot and jeans, dropping them to the floor, and slipped the fuzzy pants over legs, then tied them at the waist. The tank top came off next, she threw it across the bed, and took off her bra before putting an oversized T-shirt over her head. She left her socks on to keep her feet warm although the weather was humid. A fire in the fireplace would be romantic, but the weather wouldn't permit it right now.

Her imagination went to a big Christmas tree in the corner with a roaring fire. It would be grand to be here for Christmas. Too bad it didn't snow in Bandera. She liked snow covered hills, big trees and a warm body to curl up to. Well, she'd have the warm body this evening anyway.

She moved toward the bathroom to brush her teeth and comb out her hair before she went down to meet Joshua. Since he was taking a shower, it would be a minute or two.

Her reflection stared back from the mirror above the porcelain sink. Big green eyes with light colored eyelashes looked bright and sparkly in the light overhead. A pert little nose with freckles across the bridge was petite enough, she figured. Lips bowed into a small smile as she thought about the evening in Joshua's office. She'd never had sex on a desk before, so that was kind of interesting, but she couldn't wait to actually get him in a bed later on.

With her brush in hand, she ran it through the long, red hair, getting it shiny and soft in the process. *Leave it down or put it up?* Leaving it down sounded good. Maybe Joshua would run his fingers through it. She liked when he touched her hair.

Feeling sexy and bold, she dabbed a bit of perfume behind her ears and down her cleavage before she headed for the door to meet her cowboy. *Her cowboy. I kind of like that sentiment although I shouldn't get too attached.*

Taking the wooden steps down one at a time, she then tiptoed through the quiet lodge until she walked into the main room. The leather couches and chairs gave a homey, comfortable feel to the space. The huge rock fireplace along the back wall would allow roaring fires to heat the room to toasty in the wintertime. Bookcases flanked the fireplace with hundreds of books for the patrons to choose from if they wished to sit and read a good story. Several DVDs lined one shelf so she figured she'd check out the collection and pick something before Joshua came down.

The wind howled outside like a storm was brewing. Thunderstorms were common in Texas, she knew, but she shivered in response anyway. She loved the roll of thunder and lightning across the plains, lighting up the sky with its brightness when the rumble of thunder cracked overhead.

She glanced outside just as a crack of lightning lit up the front yard, seeing a man in a slouched cowboy hat standing on the front lawn. She hoped one of the boys wasn't out in this storm. That couldn't be a good thing. She moved closer to the window and peered out when another clap of thunder rolled across the sky. She couldn't see a thing in the pitch darkness outside.

"You okay?"

She jumped and screamed when Joshua's voice came from right behind her. "God, you scared the crap out of me."

"Sorry. I thought you heard me come down the stairs."

"No. The storm is getting loud."

"This is nothing. A small summer storm is all."

"I love summer storms. We don't get them much in California."

"I like them too." He slipped his hands around her waist, pulling her into his embrace with her back against his chest. "It's cool to stand on the porch out front and watch the rain."

"Sounds great."

"If it starts raining, we'll go out and watch the storm." He put his head on her shoulder. "What movie did you pick out?" She held up the front for him to see. "Dirty Dancing, huh? Good movie."

"Yep. I love Patrick Swayze."

Lightning flashed outside again. She could see their reflection in the window with the light behind them illuminating the main lodge room. They went together perfectly. He was quite a bit taller than her smaller frame, but she liked tall guys. It made her feel safe.

"We look pretty good together, huh?"

"Yeah. I think so too."

He rubbed his hands up and down her arms before turning her to face him. He leaned in a kissed her softly on the mouth, fitting their lips together like two puzzle pieces made for each other. It scared the hell out of her.

"I love the way you mold yourself to me when I kiss you."

"You feel good."

He smiled and brushed his lips against hers again. His tongue darted out to lick the corners of her mouth as she sighed at the touch. He knew exactly what to do to bring her to the heights of sensation with every little touch.

"I like kissing you."

"I like it too."

"Good." After another brush of his mouth over hers, he stepped back, took her hand and led her to the long leather couch facing the big screen television. "You sit. I'll put the movie in."

She watched as he approached the entertainment center housing the DVD player, game consoles, television, and stereo system. Checkered pajama bottoms molded to his nice ass just right, enhancing the visceral experience she had just looking at Joshua. She shifted on the couch trying to relieve some of the pressure in her pussy without success. She needed him to fuck her hard, but now wasn't the time or place. Soon though.

He opened the plastic container with the disc in it before pushing it into the player on the bottom. With the remote in hand, he turned to face her. His cock stood at full attention, tenting the front of his pants in the most provocative way she could ever imagine. He wanted her. Good. She wasn't alone in her needs then because good Lord she wanted him too.

"A little horny, cowboy?"

"A lot horny, little miss, but I'll keep my horny self calm until I can make love to you in a couple of hours."

"How about we skip the movie and get right to the making love part?"

He shook his head as a smile graced his lips. "Anticipation is half the fun. I know I'm anticipating lots of fun to come."

"Well, damn."

He sat next to her on the couch, wrapped an arm around her shoulders and hit play on the remote in his hand. The opening credits to the movie exploded from the speakers loud enough to wake the dead.

"Your parents are going to wake up as well as the entire household with that sound."

He pushed the button to turn the sound down to a tolerable level when the movie started to play.

For the next couple of hours, they watched one of her favorite movies and listened to the dry rumblings of the thunder and lightning outside the window. Small pings against the glass pane signaled the rain had started just as the movie was ending and her desire had reached its max with him running his fingers down her arm, playing with her hair and burying his nose in her neck. He ran soft little kisses over the surface of her shoulder in between all the other touching he was doing.

"Let's go watch the rain."

"Okay."

The ending credits continued to run on the screen while they got to their feet and walked hand in hand outside to stand on the porch. Water sluiced down the gutters, gushing out the ends into the yard. The rain sheeted sideways, pelting the concrete at their feet in huge drops. Thunder rumbled and lightning cracked in an awesome display of power no man could deny.

"Wow."

"We have some pretty spectacular storms around here."

"This is awesome."

"It is pretty cool." He stood with his back against the side of the house, cradling her in his arms in front of him so she could watch everything around her. "One of your brothers was out here earlier."

"Was he?"

"Well, I saw a cowboy standing out here. That's what I was looking at when you scared me before."

"Ah."

"It was one of your brothers, right?"

"I don't know. It could have been Cowboy Joe."

"Cowboy Joe?"

"That's what we call the cowboy who hangs around the main house. He's the ghost of a cowboy who used to live here, we figured." He shrugged his shoulders. "Someday, one of us will find out who he is I guess."

"You really should bring a medium in to see if you can cleanse the house."

"Why? We kind of like having them here. Well, except for the one starting to get a bit aggressive with me now. I might have someone see if they can do something about her. I can't have her scaring off all of my girlfriends."

"Girlfriends, as in many?"

He laughed. "Jealous?"

"Yeah. I'm your current lover. I would hope you wouldn't compare me or bring other *girlfriends* into the mix. I don't share well."

"Good." He kissed her shoulder. "Me either. I'm not a good sharer." He turned her in his arms even with the rain continuing to pound the ground in a staccato rhythm that almost sounded like drums in the faint distance. "How about we retire to upstairs? I want to make love to you properly in a real bed."

"I'd love that."

He took her hand as he pushed open the door to the lodge and moved inside. The pounding of the rain dimmed to a hum on the metal roof over their heads. He reached for the remote, and turned off the television before they headed for the stairs. Tonight would be something dreams were made of. Everything inside her told her she'd better hold on tight. This man was about to rock her world.

Joshua led her up the stairs, past her room and to the door two down from hers. When he turned the knob and pushed open the door, her breath caught in her throat. Even though they'd already had sex once before, this seemed new—different, like the first time without the raw explosiveness that this afternoon entailed. This almost brought tears to her eyes as she glanced around his space.

Typical guy's room. Dark furniture. Sturdy bedframe with a big headboard. Antique lamps gracing the nightstands. A heavy dresser against one wall with a large mirror over it reflecting back the two of them standing at the edge of his bed after he'd shut the door. They were alone in his room.

She waited with bated breath for him to touch her. His hands slowly reached out to wrap around the back of her neck and tug her to him.

"I want you."

"I'm glad because I'm on fire here."

With his hands twisted in her hair, he drew her closer until his mouth touched hers. He tasted good, like chocolate or some other decadent morsel she could totally get into. His tongue slid along her lips until they parted, waiting for the first touch, wanting him so badly, she hurt.

He brought his other hand up to cup her jaw while he devoured her mouth with soft licks, bold strokes, and devastating to her body, spearing. Her nipples stood at attention, reacting to the friction from his chest.

When he lifted his mouth, he tugged her shirt over her head, baring her breasts to his touch. "You are so beautiful, you take my breath away."

"You are good for my ego."

"I only speak the truth," he whispered, touching his forehead to hers. "I could look at you all day."

"Love on me for now. Look later."

He smiled that crooked little grin she loved. "Okay."

The touch of his lips on her breast brought her up on her toes as she cradled his head in her hands. She loved the feel of his hair through her fingers and freshly washed made it that much better. The strands were silky soft to the touch.

He'd shaved the five o'clock shadow from his cheeks for her too. She could feel the softness of his chin and cheeks on her skin as he moved from one breast to the other.

"Mmm."

"You're purring."

"I like what you are doing. Is there a problem with me purring?"

"Oh hell no. I love the sounds you make when I touch you."

His fingers worked at the tie on her pajama pants, getting it undone in record time before he pushed the material down her legs to pool at her feet. She stepped out, kicking them across the room, leaving her in nothing but a smile. Her body hummed as he stroked his hands up and down her thighs while he walked her backward until her legs touched the bed behind her.

She sat on the edge of the mattress, reaching for the waistband of his pants to free his cock from the tented material. The feel of him in her hands made her palms tingle to touch.

"Uh-uh." He pushed her hands away. "Not yet."

"I want to touch you."

"In a minute. I need to taste you first." He pushed her shoulder until she reclined on the bed. "Spread those gorgeous thighs for me, babe. I can smell you from here. I want your essence on my tongue."

She leaned back until she rested on her elbows, and spread her thighs as he crouched down on the floor between them.

The first brush of his fingers on her flesh had her moaning softly. She loved his skin against hers. He knew exactly what to do, exactly how to touch her. It was amazing how in tune he was to her body.

His nose brushed the inside of her right thigh as he kissed his way from her knee to the crease between her thigh and her pussy. He inhaled her scent like he savored everything about her for a memory later on. Would he remember her? She wondered if he would hold these hours they spent together as a beautiful thought for the years to come. It made her frown.

"What's wrong?"

"Nothing, why?"

"You're frowning. I'm down here eating you out. Frowns are not permitted."

She giggled. "Sorry. I wasn't frowning because you aren't doing everything perfectly, I just had a random thought."

"Care to share?"

"No. It's not important."

He licked her from her opening to her clit in one long stroke. She growled low in her throat at the sensation before she fully reclined on the bed and let herself enjoy the moment without thinking too hard.

When his tongue danced over the hard nub of her clit, she almost lost the hold she had on her desire. She needed this, needed him more than she ever could fathom in the darkest recesses of her mind when she's stumbled on him in the bar.

Each stroke of his tongue over her flesh brought her higher and higher until she floated amongst the clouds of her mind, envisioning spending each day doing this again and again.

He pushed both of his hands under her butt. Bringing her closer to his mouth, he flicked her clit with his tongue, ate at her flesh like a starving man, and made her explode in a kaleidoscope of colors. Ecstasy broke over her body in a mind numbing, body tingling burst of sensation she wasn't prepared for.

"Joshua!"

He brought her back down slowly with small licks and tongue flicks that had her shivering from head to toe. "Okay, stop. I can't take anymore."

"You will though. We're only getting started."

He reached over to the nightstand, pulled open the drawer and grabbed a condom. After rolling the latex down his shaft, he positioned himself between her thighs with the head of his cock at her entrance. "Are you ready for me?"

"Oh hell yeah."

He slowly pushed his hard cock into her opening, earning a deep groan from her. She loved the feel of him inside her. Every inch of his cock brought her more ecstasy than any man she'd been with before.

When he was fully inside her, he stopped, letting her adjust to the full length of him.

"Oh my God. You feel so warm, wet, and beautiful."

"I love how you fill me."

He shivered, his whole body rolling with the sensation as she wrapped her legs around his waist to bring him in even more.

When he slowly began to move inside her, the feeling drove her absolutely to the brink of insanity. His cock moved with such precision inside her flesh, he fit perfectly, too perfectly. *Lord, I need to get those thoughts out of my head.* Yes, he was good. Yes, she loved how it felt to make love with him, but good God, she couldn't think of anything past that. It wouldn't work.

He picked up his pace, driving any thoughts from her brain but how it felt to have him fuck her as he pounded into her pussy with enough force he had to hold her hips to keep her from sliding across the bed.

"Yes, yes, yes," she cried with each thrust. "Fuck me."

"Oh God," he whispered as his paced rhythm became ragged and disjointed.

She knew he was close. "I'm there. Do it."

The slapping of flesh on flesh threw her over the brink of sanity into the world where only she and

Joshua resided. He slowed his pace bringing them both gradually back to reality, a reality she wasn't sure she was ready to face.

* * * *

"Are you okay?"

"I'm perfect." Her voice sounded like the satisfied purr of a kitten.

He smiled. He liked that sound coming from her. Hell, he liked her an awful lot. "That was amazing."

"You're amazing."

"Well thank you, darlin'."

"I love when you call me, darlin'."

"How about sweetheart, babe, or dear?"

"I could go for those too."

"I like little endearments on you. They go very well." He slowly withdrew his now flaccid cock so he could dispose of the condom in the trashcan near the bed. Her sated body lying across his bed looked mighty good. He liked having her there. "How about you stand up? I'll get the covers back and we can cuddle."

"Do you like to cuddle? I mean I don't want you doing it just because you think women like it."

"I'm a cuddler from way back."

She smiled as he tugged the covers back on the bed. *Man, I really like her smile.* He loved hearing her giggle. He just plain liked her a whole lot in general, but if he didn't get his heart out of the mix, he would be in trouble when she left to go home in a couple of weeks. *Heart? What the fuck?* He didn't need that kind of complication in his life, especially with another woman and long distance. That kind of crap only led to heartache. He knew this for certain since he'd already been there, done that.

When she crawled in to the other side of his bed, she made herself comfortable on his pillow as she held out her hand for him to join her. *This could be bad.*

"Are you all right?"

"Yeah, why?"

"You look like you've got something on your mind."

"Just you."

"That's a good thing. I like being on your mind after we've made love."

Made love. Shit, when did it become making love and not having sex? "No, I'm good."

"Good. Then come in here with me. I want to run my hands all over you."

"That might lead to other things."

"Are you complaining? Because if you don't want to love on me again, just say it."

He crawled under the sheet before drawing her into his embrace, letting her rest her head on his chest. "Anytime, darlin', anytime."

"I'm glad."

He grabbed the remote to the television sitting at the end of his bed, and flipped the TV on to the news. Now that they were cuddled down beneath the sheets, warm, and satisfied sexually, he felt sleepy.

Several minutes later, he heard the soft snores of the woman in his arms as she slept soundly on his chest. He smiled while he ran his fingers up and down her arm in a soft, soothing rhythm. He liked the way she felt there. She fit nicely in his embrace, unlike any other woman he'd ever held like this.

Thoughts like this were driving him nuts. He didn't want to fall for this little bit of a woman. He couldn't. Things wouldn't work out between them, he knew from experience, but he couldn't seem to stop himself. She got under his skin more and more every day he knew her.

He might have to have a talk with his mom. She'd know what to do. She always did.

His eyelids began to get heavy, so he flipped off the television, put the remote on the nightstand and snuggled down into the bed with the gorgeous woman in his arms. He knew he'd have to distance himself soon, otherwise, he'd find himself in deeper than he ever wanted to be with another woman in his life.

Dreams haunted him while he wrestled with himself over his growing feelings for Candace. Watching Loren leave on the plane from somewhere she couldn't see him at the airport, turned into Candace before his very eyes.

He'd watched with a heavy heart as she looked over her shoulder one last time before boarding the plane back to Los Angeles. She was looking for him. Why didn't he stop her? Why would his feet not move to take her in his arms and ask her to stay? Because he couldn't, no, more like he wouldn't. She had a life in Anaheim, one he wasn't a part of, one he couldn't fathom from his experiences in life.

The traffic would drive him crazy. The people would drive him crazier. He needed his life in Bandera, the closeness of his family, the quiet of the ranch life—it was all a part of him, one he wouldn't give up for a woman—any woman.

He settled down into restless sleep for the remainder of the night even though the woman in his arms curled herself around his heart, tighter and tighter.

Morning found him spooning her back, with her leg through his and his hand resting on her breast as he slowly opened his eyes. Her hair smelled like a soft hint of the perfume still clinging to her neck near his nose. He liked the smell on her. He liked her way too much if his dream had anything to do with what was in his heart. He didn't want her to leave. He wanted to explore more with her, teach her about ranch life and the cowboy way, everything his life stood for.

"You awake?" he asked inhaling softly to bring her scent through his head.

"Mmm. Yeah." She rolled over onto her back. "I smell coffee."

"Yeah, me too.

"Are you ready for breakfast?"

His stomach growled. "I think so."

"Me too. I need to stop at my room and shower though. I'll meet you down there in fifteen?"

"Sure. I'll have the coffee waiting. How do you take yours?"

"Cream and sugar."

"Okay. I'll find us a table. They might already be serving. If they are, I'll grab you a plate."

"Perfect." She leaned up and kissed him on the mouth softly before jumping up and tossing her clothes on. "Be there in a few," she said, opening his door.

She swept out like a whirlwind, closing it behind her as he leaned back in the bed with his hands behind his head. What was he going to do about his growing feelings for her? He didn't need this complication in their relationship. It was supposed to be a fun few weeks, not anything serious.

"I'm just going to play it by ear. There isn't anything I can do at this point anyway. If things work out, they work out. If she leaves and I never hear from her again, I'll make it through just like I did with Loren."

After all, the two women were the same in what they wanted, right? His heart didn't figure into the equation of their lives.

Man, I'm so screwed.

Chapter Eight

I love this! Mud splashed the bottom of her jeans, spraying everywhere as one of Joshua's brothers raced through the mud hole with his truck. Nothing like a good mudding party from what Joshua told her, to set her heart free.

He said this was what they did on a Saturday afternoon or evening before they went to the bar, got liquored up and went home at the wee hours of the morning. Tonight, she would spend the night in his arms again, loving him until the early morning, she decided.

She was slowly becoming a little too addicted to the kind of man Joshua Young represented. Right now, she couldn't even remember what men in California looked like.

Her cell phone jingled on her hip, bringing her thoughts back to the work she needed to do. Her vice president of sales called her earlier in the day to tell her they had a problem with one of the computer programs she'd written recently, and she had to deal with it—today.

Putting off work while on vacation, what a concept. *Damn, I don't want to deal with this. Why in hell couldn't he?*

"What?" she barked into the phone.

"Sorry, boss. I needed to tell you we need you to write the patch for the program by tomorrow, so we can get it out to the buyers. This is bad."

She began pacing back and forth, her feet squishing in the mud under her boots without caring what it did to her pant legs. "I said I'll take care of it and I will. I'm on vacation, remember?"

"Yeah, I know."

She tipped her head back on her shoulders, swearing under her breath. "Why can't you handle this?"

"It's your program, Candace. I don't have the coding memorized like you do. It would take me days to write the patch where it will take you a couple of hours."

Sighing, she rolled her eyes and glanced at the gorgeous man across the mud hole from her getting ready to jump into his truck for his next turn at the hole. She liked watching from outside more than she liked sitting in the cab or driving. She'd done both. Joshua had actually let her drive his truck! Shock, she knew. Cowboys didn't let *anyone* drive their truck. "Fine. I'll get it done by tomorrow. You'll have it in your email in the morning."

"Perfect. Thanks."

"Just take care of the office, Aaron. I need your expertise in other areas. I'll handle the coding."

"Have fun on your vacation."

"I would if you would quit calling me with this shit."

"I love you too, Candace."

"It's a good thing you are my brother, asshole."

"Smooches, babe. Enjoy your cowboy."

"How'd you know I'd hooked up with a cowboy?"

"Because I know my little sister like the back of my hand. You can't handle being around all that

testosterone without falling for one. Just don't bring
one home, will you?"

"No problem."

"Have you seen much of our ex-brother-in-law?"

"Not much. I spent the first few days with him, and
I'll see him this evening for dinner before I hit the bar,
but other than that, no."

"I thought you were there to visit Arnold?"

"Yeah, well, plans have changed."

"Hmm."

"Back off, Aaron. I'm living my life, and I intend
to have fun while doing it."

"Good. You were in too much of a funk before you
went out there. Just don't fall in love with one of those
Wrangler wearing, cowboy hat types."

"Me?"

"Yeah, you. I know how you are."

"Maybe."

"Look. I'm all for you finding someone to spend
the rest of your life with, but a cowboy? Really?"

"I like cowboys."

"I know you do or do now."

"Well, no worries. The one here doesn't want a
permanent relationship and long distance ones don't
work."

"True."

"Dude, I'm a California girl from the top of my
head to the tips of my sandals. I'm not giving up my
life there, no matter how gorgeous the guy is."

"Good to know."

"I'll talk to you later. I'm in the middle of a mud
bath at the moment."

"Mud bath?"

"Yeah, the family has taken me out to go muddin'."

"What the hell is muddin'?"

"I'll tell you about it when I get home. It's great fun. Lots of big trucks, mud, water and dirt. You would enjoy it."

"Somehow, I don't think so."

"Yeah, probably not with your Armani suit and spit-shined shoes."

"Yeah, I don't like to get dirty."

"I didn't think I did either, until now."

"Well, have fun, and I'll see you in a week."

"Wow. Have I been here two weeks already?"

"Yes ma'am, you have, and I, for one, can't wait until you get back."

"See you soon."

"Bye."

She hung up her phone as Joshua spun through the mud hole, sloshing more mud on her jeans. She laughed at the grin on his face when he waved from the driver's seat. Men and their toys. Why did it seem like he was having more fun than she was standing out there with mud to her ankles. Yes, she needed to write the code for the patch, but for now, she planned to have a little more fun before supper.

Joshua parked his mud covered truck off to the side as she watched his other brothers do the same run he'd done a few minutes ago.

When he sauntered closer, he smiled that lip-tilting smile of his that made her panties soaked. She'd spent the better part of the past two weeks in bed, in the barn, at the pond, at the bar and wherever else they could think of loving and living his lifestyle. No, she wasn't ready to go home.

They sat out on the porch rocking chairs just talking like an old married couple, laughing at stories of their childhood, sharing events of their lives, and just soaking up being together.

She sure would miss him when she had to go home in a week, but for now, she would enjoy being with him before her time on the ranch came to a close.

Tonight, they would drink, dance, and love the night away.

He grabbed her around the waist, hefting her into his arms and then strolling toward the mud hole.

"What are you doing?"

"Getting you thoroughly into the party."

"I'm already muddy."

"Not sufficiently. You need a mud bath."

"Joshua, put me down."

"Nope."

"Baby, I don't need mud in my underwear, I need you."

"But it'll be fun cleaning out those spots later in the shower we share. We haven't had shower sex yet."

"Joshua, please." She screeched as he strode right into the mud hole to his knees, and then took her down with him in a splash of water and dirt, sending her under the brown goop. She came back up with brown water streaming down her cheeks after she brushed her wet, dirty hair out of her face. "Oh my God! I don't believe you did that."

He laughed before he leaned in and kissed her full on the mouth. "You look fabulous!"

Not one to be bested, she climbed to her feet and dove at him, knocking him back into the mud until he was covered from head to toe thoroughly as well. His hat floated by. Good thing it was straw and could easily be cleaned, otherwise, she figured he'd have been pissed. *Oh well, he started it.*

She laughed as he came up sputtering. A glob of goop stuck to the top of his head until she took pity on him, reached over and brushed it off. "You look fabulous too!"

Thank goodness he was a good sport, even though he was the one who shoved her into the mud first.

When he climbed to his feet, water and mud sloshed off his tall frame to splash around him. "I'm ready for a shower, some sex, supper, and a beer, not necessarily in that order."

"Good, me too."

He tossed her over his shoulder and headed toward his truck.

"Put me down!"

"Nope. I am going to take advantage of the shower with you."

"But you'll get your truck seats all muddy."

"They're leather. They'll wash."

After he opened the door, he put her on the seat, kissed her on the mouth, and then shut the door. She couldn't help but admire the gorgeous man he was as he walked around the front of the vehicle to climb into the driver's side.

"You're grinning."

"I like the way you look even covered in mud. Is that a crime to grin about?"

His grin matched the one she knew lifted the corners of her mouth. "Nope. Otherwise, they'd be hauling me off too, because I like the way you look too."

"I can't wait to get you in the shower. I hope it's a big stall because I plan on rinsing you clean and then sucking you dry."

"Damn, woman."

"Just thought I'd let you know my plan."

"Good plan."

"I like it."

He kicked up dry dust and dirt as he sped back to the house in record time, bouncing and bumping along the rutted road. It was a good thing she had her seatbelt on, otherwise, she'd have a headache from hitting her head on the ceiling of his truck.

"In a hurry, big boy?"

"You bet. My girl said she was going to suck me dry. I'm in a damn big hurry."

She laughed out loud, snorting in her guffaws of laughter as she covered her nose and mouth.

The moment they hit the parking lot at the main lodge, he had the truck off, the door open and ran around to the passenger side to get to her. She giggled hysterically when he pulled her door open, threw her over his shoulder and ran for the house.

"Gang way! Woman in my arms," he shouted as he ran for the stairs.

Laughing, she bounced against his shoulder, her hair in a stringy mess down his back with her butt in the air. She didn't even think he shut the driver's or passenger's door on his truck in his haste to get her naked.

The minute he had her in his room, he slammed the door and started working on her clothes.

"Easy, cowboy. I can get it."

"But I can do it better," he said, whipping the shirt over her head and then shoving her pants down her legs. "See?"

"You need to be naked too."

"Okay. I can handle that." In seconds, he stood in front of her, naked as the day he was born.

"Nice." She wrapped her hand around his straining cock. "Shower?"

"Yep." He swung her up in his arms and headed for the bathroom at a quick pace.

The shower stall was something out of a home improvement shop. It was bigger than the one in her room and made of solid glass. She loved how the showerheads came out in several directions, soaking a body and massaging it at the same time. "I love your shower."

"Since I've been living in this room for several years, I had Mom and Dad customize it for me."

"Didn't you ever want a room out in one of the cabins?"

"Sometimes, but I like this one the best."

He set her down on her feet before he reached in and turned the spigot on. Water shot out from several directions when she stepped into the glass enclosure, humming her appreciation. Warmth cascaded over her hair and shoulders, washing the mud and grime from her body as Joshua stood at the back of the stall admiring the view, from what she could tell. "What?"

"I like watching you. You're gorgeous."

"Thanks, cowboy."

"No problem, darlin'."

She reached over and grabbed some shampoo to soap her hair, lathering her scalp until it tingled.

"Can I help?"

"Sure." She turned around so he could scrub her hair before she turned back around to rinse.

The water flowed down her body, washing away the mud, but not completely. A moment later, she felt his hands on her breasts, soaping and scrubbing her nipples until they were squeaky clean. "I think those are clean enough."

"I'll be the judge of that."

His mouth found her left nipple, sucking it between his lips until she came up on her toes. "So good." When he lifted his head, he soaped the rest of her body with the aloe scented soap until every spot was more than clean. "Your turn," she said, taking some soap between her hands and lathering it up well while he rinsed the mud from his body under the water spray. She ran her hands down his chest, across his six-pack abs and down to his cock. The hard flesh stood proud and waiting as she ran her soapy hands around and around.

"You're gonna kill me."

"Yep."

She bent down, running her hands down his thighs, around his calves, across his ankles to between his toes. He chuckled when she soaped each toe clean before working her way back up the back of his calves, thighs and buttocks. God, she loved his butt. In or out of Wranglers, she didn't care. He had a nice ass.

After she thoroughly soaped his butt, she ran her hands over the straining muscles of his back, rubbing and pushing her hands into the hard flesh. He groaned, dropping his head forward to his chest as she kneaded every ridge and plain of his back.

"You have a magnificent body."

"Thanks, darlin'."

He turned back around to face her, his eyes bright with desire. "I want you."

"You'll have me, but first I promised to suck you dry." She dropped back to her knees. Taking his cock in her hand, she bent forward to encircle his cockhead with her mouth.

"Oh fuck."

She licked around the underside of the head before pushing the entire length of him into her mouth and humming her appreciation. It wasn't easy, but she inhaled through her nose until she could take all of him into her mouth.

The musky smell of his groin made her throbbing pussy wetter as she slid closer so she could lick and suck until he came in her mouth.

He fisted her hair in his hands as she bobbed her head up and down, slipping and sliding his cock in and out of her mouth while she massaged his balls with her other hand.

"I'm gonna come."

"Mmm." She grabbed both of his butt cheeks in her hands to keep him close as his hips pumped several more times before hot, salty cum shot down her throat.

"Fuck." He stumbled back, taking his cock from between her lips, and slumped against the cold tile of the shower. "That was amazing."

"Told you I'd suck you dry."

"And you did, darlin'. I haven't had such a great blow job in, oh, I don't know, ever?"

She stood, dragging her tongue up his abdomen, across his pecs, up his neck to his waiting mouth.

He wrapped his hands in her wet hair, fisting it until it stung her scalp. "You are…I can't even think of the word."

"That's good enough for me."

"Are we done in here?"

"No. I want you to fuck my ass."

"Seriously?"

"Yeah."

"I don't have any lube in here, and I think a dry run would hurt like a bitch."

"Okay, we'll wait until we get in the bedroom. I don't want to use soap."

"No, that would hurt too."

"You'll do this for me?"

"Oh hell yeah. I love ass sex."

"Good. Me too."

He shut the shower off, grabbed a towel from the rack and dried her from head to toe with soft, tantalizing strokes across her breasts, down between her legs and across her butt. It didn't matter. She was already ready to explode with a mere touch of his hands on her skin, but she didn't. She wanted to feel his cock in her ass.

After he dried himself off, he wrapped the towel around his waist and led her into the bedroom. She didn't know why he bothered with the towel until she realized they might need something to clean up with after all was said and done.

He spread the towel on the bed. "Bend over the bed on your stomach."

"Will you eat me out first?"

"Sure, darlin'. I love your taste."

"Good grief, you make me so wet." She glanced down at his cock as it started to get hard again. He sure didn't need much time to recuperate. "Are you horny again?"

"I'm forever horny around you."

She laid back on the bed, reclining against the pillows so it lifted her back up enough she could watch him between her legs. The sight was amazing to see with his dark curls buried there. It made her pussy throb just to think about it.

At the first touch of his tongue on her clit, she moaned softly. The bristle of his whiskers against her pussy lips scraped deliciously on her skin, enhancing the feel of his mouth on her. She loved when he did this.

After several minutes of licking, sucking, and biting her clit and pussy, he shoved two fingers deep inside her, throwing her into a screaming, color-exploding orgasm meant to rock her world. It did. He did.

"Now," he said, sitting up and leaning over to pull open the nightstand drawer. He pulled out a tube of lubrication and a condom as he got ready to prepare her for his penetration. "You've done this before, I take it."

"Oh yeah."

"Do you enjoy anal?"

"It's one of my favorites."

"Good. Mine too, and I'll love having you squeeze me so tight when you come, I'll explode myself."

She turned over onto her stomach, resting her head on her arms, waiting for him to spread the lube around her anus. When his slick fingers penetrated her ass, she sucked in a ragged breath and blew it out. Even though she loved anal sex, it had been awhile since she trusted a man enough to let him at that dark hole.

"Easy."

"Sorry. It stings a bit."

"Been awhile?"

"Yeah. I haven't been with anyone I trusted enough to do this."

"Thank you."

"For?"

"Trusting me."

"You mean a lot to me, Joshua."

"You mean a lot to me too."

It was the best she could do at this point. She didn't want to admit anything more because it would mean leaving it behind when she went home in a week, and that would break her heart.

Several minutes later, he'd rubbed enough lube into her ass to make her slick to his touch. He'd also did some slow fingering of her clit and pussy to bring her back to the brink of climax until he was ready to ride her ass. As he got behind her and his cock nudged at her back hole, she widened her knees and pushed back against him. The slow glide of his cock into her had her moaning at a high pitch until his groin met her ass cheeks.

"Ah, hell yeah."

"You feel fantastic."

She panted hard trying to keep her climax at bay until he started to move. *Holy hell, it felt amazing having him there.* "Move please. I'm going to die if you don't fuck me."

He began a slow glide in and out, in and out. Her pussy throbbed with her racing heart as her body climbed higher on that plain of ecstasy she craved with her next breath. When he picked up the pace, she teetered on the edge of insanity while she pushed back against his thrusting hips to get every inch of length he could give her.

"Joshua!" She knew she screamed loud enough the entire house had to hear her, but she didn't care right at the moment. She just hoped they were all out and about on the ranch somewhere rather than in their rooms.

"Oh God. Oh God." His panting chant echoed in her ear while he continued to thrust in an uncoordinated rhythm until he groaned with his own climax a few moments later. "Wow."

"Yeah, wow."

He slowly withdrew from her before heading into the bathroom to clean up. She collapsed on the bed in a boneless heap until he returned a couple of minutes later, chuckling to himself. "You look well satisfied."

"Oh, I am. Thank you."

"You're welcome." She felt a warm washcloth caress her folds as he clean her up from front to back.

"You didn't have to do that. I could have managed."

"I wanted to."

"You are one amazing man, Joshua Young."

Chapter Nine

Music poured from the bar as they drove into a parking spot at The Dusty Boot later that evening. She wanted to spend as much time as possible with Joshua before she had to leave, and dancing with the gorgeous cowboy fit right into those plans. Making love with him had been the highlight of her trip to Bandera, but getting to know him on a personal level made the trip worthwhile.

"Is Arnold going to be here tonight? I know you talked to him earlier."

"Yeah, he said he would stop by. He wants to check on me." She dropped her gaze to her lap. "I feel bad. I was supposed to be here visiting him, and all I've done is spend time with you."

"Maybe you should spend the next week at his place."

"Maybe, but then I wouldn't see you."

"No, you wouldn't."

She didn't like that idea at all. Caring for this rugged cowboy had become part of her, and she wasn't sure what to do about it. She wouldn't call it love. Nope, it couldn't be that because she couldn't handle falling in love with him and leaving him behind when she went back to California and to her boring life.

He brought her hand to his mouth, kissing the back before letting her go so he could open her door. *Man, I love the chivalry of the southern gentleman. They have this shit down pat.* He opened her door and took her hand to help her down since she'd worn a short little jean skirt with her cowboy boots just like the other women in Texas. Impressively, she'd even broken her boots in during her stay in the state. How would her staff like it if she started wearing them to the office every day? They were really comfortable once she got them broke in.

Joshua slipped his arm around her shoulders after he shut the truck door to escort her into the bar. It was busy, but then again, she figured it would be on a Saturday night. "Are your brothers here?"

"Some of them. You can't have a bar on Saturday without at least one Young brother in it in Bandera."

She smiled knowing he spoke the truth. She'd learned that about his family over the course of her time on the ranch. They loved each other with a fierceness unsurpassed in any family she'd had the privilege to know in her lifetime, and she envied them that closeness even though she had a great family of her own. They did for one another. They had a bond that she couldn't quite fathom on her own, but one she hoped someday to experience for herself with a man she'd chosen to spend the rest of her life with.

They walked through the double doors to be enveloped in the crowd of people milling and moving about. The dance floor was packed while the band played a quick two-step number. Luckily, Joshua was tall so he could see over most of the crowd to find the table his brothers had secured in the back corner.

"There they are. Let's go."

With her hand in his, he led them through the throngs of people until the crowd parted near the back and she could see Jackson, Joey, Jonathan, Joel, Mesa, Jason, Paige, Jeremiah, Callinda, Jacob, and Peyton in the huge booth. The only brother missing was Jeff, and he was at home with Terri and the new baby. "Wow. What a crowd."

They'd pushed several tables together to seat them all.

Candace glanced around the bar. A sea of cowboy hats could be seen between her and the door to the outside. The place was definitely hopping tonight. The band rocked it on stage while a group of people did the two-step in a wave around the dance floor. She tapped her foot to the music as she watched with a little envy.

"Care to dance?"

"I'd love to." Joshua led her out to the dance floor where they found a small spot to get into the group of dancers, then he pulled her close. "I think there is supposed to be a little more room between us when we two-step."

"Not in my book."

She laughed while he led her around the floor. "You're a good dancer."

"One cannot be a cowboy and not know how to at least two-step. Not in Texas anyway."

"Tis true."

They shuffled around the floor several times as the beat of the music pounded so hard, it felt like her heart would beat out of her chest to the rhythm they were keeping. The band was wonderful. Some of the best sound she'd heard in several years.

As the two-step song came to an end, they wound down into a slow beat. Joshua tugged her in until she rested her head against his chest. She didn't realize the differences in their height until he pulled her in. He was a tall man compared to her smaller frame. Being only five-foot-five, he towered over her, his six foot plus size frame making her feel tiny beside him.

"What are you thinking about?"

"You."

"Are you now?"

"Yep."

"And what are you thinking about me?"

"How much I want to spread you out on my bed, kiss you from head to toe, and make love to you more than anything in this world."

"We just did that earlier."

"Yeah, but I want to do it again and again."

"I'm game, cowboy."

He inhaled through his nose and exhaled on a rush. "I'm not going to take you to bed again tonight. We are going to enjoy ourselves with friends and family, dance, drink, have a good time, get a little wild, and whatever else you want to do. How about a little star gazin'?"

"Sounds romantic." She ran a fingernail down his chest until it reached his belt buckle. "Are you a romantic guy?"

"I like to think so."

She glanced up through her lashes, giving him a smile she hoped came across as a little flirty and a whole lot sexy. "Well for now, how about we end this song, get a beer, tequila, whiskey…whatever and shoot the shit with your family?"

"Sounds like a plan."

"I may even let you do body shots off me."

One eyebrow rose as he looked down at her. "I like the sound of that." His gaze rested on her cleavage. Her nipples pebbled at the heat in his eyes. "I really, really like the sound of that."

"I bet you do, cowboy." She ran a finger from her ear to a sensitive spot between her breasts. "Lick a little salt off my neck, then down the shot of tequila resting between my breasts?" She sighed, thinking about his tongue on her skin.

"I'm gettin' hard thinkin' about all of that lovely flesh beneath my tongue."

"Mmm. I'm wet thinking about you all over me." She pulled his head down so she could whisper in his ear. "How your cock felt riding my ass."

"Keep this up, babe, and we won't be doin' much socializing. I'll take you home and ride you again."

"Promise?"

"Oh yeah, but we said we were going to have a good time tonight."

"Riding me isn't a good time?"

"Hell yeah, it is, but I want more from you than just fuckin'."

"But I like fuckin'."

"Me too, especially with you. You wanted to experience everything cowboy. I aim to provide you with as much experience as you can get crammed into your time here in Bandera. This includes two-steppin', drinkin' beer, and living the cowboy lifestyle which means The Dusty Boot on the weekends."

"Party pooper." She stuck her lip out in a little pout as he laughed.

"We'll get to the other soon enough, darlin'."

"Promise?"

"Oh, yeah."

The song came to an end, slowly drifting off on a long, mournful pluck of the strings on the steel guitar. She wasn't sure, but she thought her heart skipped a beat when she glanced up into Joshua's eyes. His face turned serious for a moment. He almost looked melancholy.

"We should get a drink."

"Okay," she said as he took her hand to lead her off the dance floor.

They came around the corner of the divider right into the arms of a petite brunette. "Joshua."

"Loren."

The woman looked Candace up one side and down the other. "It's nice to see you."

"Yeah."

She could feel the chill from across the room. Was this the someone Joshua referred to as a girlfriend? Did she want to find out? "Hi. I'm Candace."

"Loren."

"What are you doing here? I thought you were in New York."

"I came home."

"Came home?"

"Yeah, as in moved back to Bandera."

"Why?"

"I missed my family."

"Oh yeah?"

"And you."

Candace felt Joshua go totally stiff. So, this was the *girlfriend* he mentioned, and she totally wanted back into his life if she was any judge of people.

"Can we talk somewhere?"

"No."

"You won't even talk to me, Joshua, after all we meant to each other?"

"I never meant shit to you. Not enough to give up New York. We were over a long time ago, Loren, get over it."

"Are you over it?"

"Yeah, I am."

Loren stepped closer, edging out Candace for the spot next to Joshua. Candace's neck hair rose to stand on end. *Oh no, she didn't just push me out of the way!*

"I don't think you are."

Candace rose to her full height, stepping between Loren and Joshua. "Okay, listen bitch. He said he's done. Back off. He's with me tonight. You two can figure this out at a later time. Right now, this is me time."

"Who the fuck are you?"

"His new girlfriend, and trust me, you don't want to mess with me."

"You aren't from around here."

"Nope. I'm from Los Angeles, and I know how to take down puny girls like you."

Loren stepped back. "Joshua?"

"I'm with Candace. I don't have time for you and your games anymore, Loren. Go break someone else's heart. You won't get mine again." He wrapped his arm around her shoulder and walked them back to where his family sat in the corner. The whole group sat silently watching the exchange between their brother and his ex. "Who's buying? I need some salt and a tequila shot to take off my hot date. She promised."

She knew she'd do anything to make him forget the little brunette bimbo who stood nearby watching him with hot eyes. "Yes, I did. Bring it on, cowboy."

Jacob signaled for the waitress who hurried over within minutes. He ordered drinks for everyone including the tequila for her and Joshua. She couldn't wait to get his tongue on her skin.

When the waitress arrived with their drinks, Joshua ordered another round immediately, to keep them in liquor.

She got the impression it would be a hug the commode kind of night.

* * * *

Joshua didn't like the way his gaze kept wandering back to where Loren stood against the wall watching him with Candace. He didn't want to focus on her or the way she looked tonight. His date was with Candace. The waitress brought another shot of tequila. He'd lost count of how many he'd drank, but as far as he was concerned, it wasn't enough.

"Are you okay?" she asked, touching his cheek.

"Yeah. I'm just not drunk enough yet."

She reached up and kissed him on the lips before wiping her lipstick from his mouth. "Don't let her get to you."

"It's not easy."

"I know."

"You've been there?"

"Sort of. I had a fiancé once. I caught him with his secretary doing it on his desk in my own office. We worked together at my company. I found out he was only after the money and name."

"I'm sorry." He felt bad. She'd been through her own kind of hell with a man, and here he was dumping his problem with Loren on her shoulders. She didn't need that. It wasn't fair to her to be second best at any time, but especially tonight. His focus should be on her, not how his ex dumped him like a hot rock the moment the bright lights of New York blinded her to his love.

She shrugged as she fingered the buttons on the front of his shirt. "It's okay. It was a while ago, but it still hurts sometimes, and it sure makes it hard to trust anyone again."

"It sure does."

She sprinkled some salt on her neck, bent her head to the side. "Lick away, cowboy."

"You know. I don't usually drink tequila."

"You're doing pretty fabulous with it tonight."

"I'm a beer kind of cowboy."

"Would you rather I put a beer bottle between my breasts?"

"I'd take anything between your gorgeous tits."

"Use me."

"What?"

She grabbed him behind the head and brought his lips to hers. "I want you to take me out to your truck, fuck me under the stars and use me to get over her. She's not for you. If she was willing to leave you like that, she's not the woman you need to be with. You need to find someone who will love you for yourself, everything you are, and whatever life brings you. Find someone who will be your everything."

"Will you?"

"I can't promise forever. You know that."

"I don't need forever right now, but I need you."

"You have me for however long you need me, Joshua."

He leaned in, bringing their mouths together in a hot kiss. All thoughts of Loren seeped from his mind at the touch of Candace's mouth. He knew her. He wanted her. She was his…for now.

When he finally came up for air, her eyes were bright with desire as they met his. "Shall we go outside? I want to show you the stars."

"Sounds like a plan to me."

He turned to his brothers, said their goodbyes and then headed for the door. The sea of people parted before them without much preamble.

The cooler air of the evening hit him in the face as he opened the door to The Dusty Boot, leaving Loren and her gaze behind. He was done thinking about her and what she'd done to his heart. Moving on became his mantra. He'd start with giving into his desires and need for Candace.

With her hand in his, he led her to the truck, opened the door and then lifted her inside with a hand on each side of her waist. He loved the feel of her body under his touch. She was perfect, at least for him anyway.

"Where are we going?"

"Out to do a little stargazin'."

Smiling, she settled herself into the leather seats of his truck, her booted feet tapped out a rhythm to the song on the radio.

Why he liked her, he wasn't sure. She wasn't his type of woman, really. She didn't do the cowboy thing very well, but she tried, and she seemed to be enjoying everything he was showing her. She cleaned up real nice with her cowboy gear. The short little jean skirt showed off her assets nicely.

They drove in silence down the darkened streets of Bandera, down the paved road leading out to their ranch. He had the perfect spot to show her. It was a hill on their property where you could see for miles. The sleeping bag in the back of his truck would support their bodies and cushion the soft spots from the hard bed. Four wheel drive on his truck would be required to get there, but he didn't mind.

"Is this a special spot?"

"Yep."

"So I'm kinda special?"

He took her hand and brought it to his lips for a kiss on her fingers. "You sure are, darlin'."

A half sliver of moon reflected silver beams off everything around them as they bounced up the gravel road toward the top of the hill. Little did she know, but this was his favorite spot on the ranch. It might be because it was all his. He owned this little track of land given to him by his parents when he turned eighteen. He hoped someday to put his permanent house up here so he could look out over the hills around his family home and dream about his future.

As they rounded a bend in the road, the scenery was revealed. Junipers, rocks, and scrub brush stretched for miles. In the spring, bluebonnets bloomed in masses up here. Below, to the left was a pasture area where he would build his barn. His house, of course, would go on the hill. The plans were already in his head. A long porch to put a couple of rocking chairs on, a big kitchen for his wife to cook in, a giant master bedroom for their huge bed, a wonderful bathroom with a great soaking tub and a shower immense enough for them to take intimate showers together.

One thing he couldn't figure out though. Why did all of his plans now include Candace? She wasn't for him, right? She had her life in California. She'd already made it clear there wasn't anything for them on a long-term basis, but he sure had it bad for her even in the short time she'd been around. How would he feel in a few weeks?

He parked his truck and turned to face her. "What do you think?"

Her mouth hung open in awe. "Oh my. This is absolutely gorgeous, Joshua." She slowly opened the door before sliding out and closing it behind her.

He came around the front of the truck a minute later to stand beside her on the knoll overlooking the back part of Thunder Ridge.

"The stars look close enough to touch."

"I love it up here. I plan to build my house on this very hill, someday."

"This is yours?"

"Yeah. Our parents gave us each a chunk of land when we turned eighteen. This is mine."

"I could totally see you sitting up here with your family running around or when you're old in your rocking chair, a grandkid on your knee."

"I have the same picture in my head."

"It bet it's a big, beautiful house. Log with a great big fireplace in the living room for the chilly winters." She spun around with her arms wide. "The stars above shining through a big skylight in the bedroom so you can see them every night." Her spinning stopped as she wobbled a little. "Now I'm dizzy."

"Here. Sit on this rock with me." He pulled her into his arms, sitting her on his left knee while he rested on the rock he sat on every time he came up here to dream about his future. He thought it kind of poignant that he'd never brought another woman up here.

The smell of her perfume drifted to him, making him want to bury his nose in her neck. She smelled fantastic. The scent subtle, but intoxicating to his senses. He skimmed his fingers down her arm in a slow motion meant to soothe, although it was driving him sexually insane at the same time.

"Better?

"Yeah. I guess I shouldn't have done that with alcohol in me. Not good for my head."

"Let's grab the sleeping bags out of the back of my truck, spread them out on the bed and we'll watch the stars."

"Cool."

Once they had the stuff out of the rear part of the cab of his truck, they spread them out in the bed, threw the pillows near the top and climbed in. He leaned back against the pillows before bringing her into his arms to rest her head in the crook of his shoulder. *Now this is the life.*

"This is perfect," she whispered as she put her hand on his chest.

"You wanted everything cowboy. This is one of my favorite pastimes."

"How many women have you brought up here?"

"None."

She sat straight up in shock, cocking her head to the side. "What? None?"

"Just you."

"Seriously?"

"Yeah."

"Why?"

"Why what?"

"Why me?"

"I like you."

She curled back into his arms as she said, "I'm sure you've liked others. What about that woman at the bar? Loren?"

"I never brought her up here."

"Why not? You loved her, right?"

"Yeah. At least, I thought I did. I'm beginning to wonder if that's the emotion that was involved though."

"I don't understand."

His fingers did a slow crawl on her arm, as he loved the feeling of her skin under his touch. She had such soft skin. "Seeing her tonight hurt, but I'm not sure it was pain from her walking away from me when I thought we were in love or just jealousy because she chose to move without even talking to me about it."

"She didn't even tell you about it?"

"Not until the day before she was supposed to be in New York. I found out from one of my brothers. She wasn't even going to tell me, she said."

"Wow."

"Yeah."

"I would never do that to a guy I loved."

"I don't think you would. You seem to be a straight shooting kind of girl."

"I try."

A shooting star zipped across the sky. "Did you make a wish on the star?"

"Yeah."

"Me too."

"What was your wish?"

"I can't tell you. It won't come true that way."

"Oh." She sat up and looked into his eyes. "I wished this night would go on forever, but since it's impossible, I figured I could tell you."

He pushed his hand into the hair at her temple, bringing her mouth down to his. He couldn't tell her, he'd wished for the same thing.

Chapter Ten

The rise and fall of his chest beneath her cheek and the slow thudding of his heartbeat in her ear, made her sigh.

She couldn't help it. She was falling deeply for this man, and it was all wrong. Love with a cowboy didn't fit in her lifestyle. Texas didn't work for her. She had her family and her business in California. Besides, she didn't think he cared for her in a permanent sort of way. He was still hooked on Loren, from what she could tell, and she wasn't one to play second fiddle to anyone.

His lips brushed across her forehead, sending tingles down her arms. He seemed to care for her, a little anyway, but one couldn't make a relationship work long distance and only based on liking. Love had to be shared to work. She'd found that out the hard way with her ex.

Catching him with his secretary hurt. When she realized he was only after her money and name, that hurt worse than his infidelity. The leggy blonde he'd been doing on his desk, didn't surprise her really. Their love life had taken a stagnant turn. She wanted a little more adventure in their sex, he wanted missionary. She wanted toys, he wanted wham bam thank you ma'am, nothing like making love with Joshua. Her cowboy worshipped her body with his lips and tongue when they'd come together. *My cowboy? Well, yeah, I guess so.* She could think of him as her cowboy if she wanted to while she was here. After all, he did belong to her for the time being.

She slipped two buttons free on the front of his shirt, before sliding her hand between the parted material. His warm skin made her girly parts come alive with a rush of blood. She wanted him more than anything in the world. Would he make love under the stars? Could she give him something to remember her by while she was here? She hoped so, she didn't want him to forget her easily.

Tipping her head back on his bicep, she could see his profile in the moonlight. Strong jaw, full lips, whiskered cheek with the shadow of his unshaven jaw, straight nose, a wisp of dark hair falling across his brow…he almost looked like a young boy until he turned toward her, and the heated gaze met hers.

"I said we weren't going to make love tonight, but I want you out here under the stars."

"I want that too," she whispered, bringing their lips within a hairsbreadth of each other. "Make love to me, Joshua. I need to feel you inside me."

He slowly undressed her, his hands like silk upon her skin.

When she was finally lying beneath him completely naked, she reached her hands up to encircle his neck as he slowly brought their bodies together. The feel of him inside her, made her squirm. She needed to feel everything, every slide of his cock, every touch of his fingers, and every brush of his lips on hers. I love you tingled on her lips while tears gathered in her eyes.

"Why are you crying? I'm not hurting you, am I?"

Unable to answer without bursting into tears, she shook her head no and buried her face in his neck. He didn't love her. She knew that. Cowboys didn't fall in love with city girls.

"God, you feel amazing."

She wrapped her legs around his waist, taking every inch of him into her body. The slow slide of his cock in and out had her moaning softly.

When he slipped his hands beneath her shoulders and brought her into an upright position, she wasn't sure what he planned until his cock went deeper. "Fuck."

"Oh yeah. Ride me, Candace."

The rocking of her hips brought them to the brink of an explosive climax within minutes. He growled in her ear how good she felt, how much he wanted her, and how he wished this moment could go on forever. She wished it too, as she rode herself into an earth shattering climax. The cry of his name on her lips and his answering moan of hers coming from his mouth, made her smile is satisfaction. She'd given that to him.

"You're perfect."

"Thank you. You are pretty special yourself, cowboy."

"Oh shit."

"What?"

"We forgot the condom."

"No worries. I'm on the pill."

His sigh of relief had her wondering if he thought she would try to trap him into a relationship with a baby. The last thing she needed right now would be a pregnancy to complicate things.

"I'm clean."

"Me too."

"Thank the Lord."

She leaned back in his arms so she could look into his gaze. "I would never try to trap you into a relationship, Joshua. I don't want babies yet."

"I didn't think you would, but it is always a concern."

"Why?"

"I'm not sure I even want kids, but definitely not now."

"Then we are on the same page."

"Yeah, I guess we are."

She rose up on her knees, forcing his softening cock to slide out of her body. This conversation bothered her, and she wasn't quite sure why. Nothing prepared her for his immediate response to the no condom thing. She kind of liked the feel of his bare cock inside her pussy and hoped they could do it again, but if his opinion of her was so low he thought she would manipulate him, he didn't know her very well.

"What's wrong?" he asked, sliding his pants back on over his hips. "Whatever I did, I'm sorry."

She resnapped her bra behind her back before slipping on her shirt. "I'm upset you would even think that low of me."

"I don't."

"Then why the big sigh? Has someone tried to trap you before with a pregnancy?"

"No, but Jeff kind of was with his first wife, and then she screwed around on him the night of their wedding. He really loved her, and she treated him like shit."

"I'm not her."

"I know you aren't, but really, I don't know you all that well. We've known each other for only a short time. I'm not saying you would do anything that underhanded."

Great, he thinks I'm a lying, conniving slut! "I appreciate your words. Really, I do."

"Why are you mad?"

"Because deep down you don't trust women."

"No, I don't. Not really. Every woman I've known, outside of my mother, has tried getting to one of us through manipulation in one form or another."

She stomped her foot back into her right boot. "What about your sisters-in-law? Surely you don't think they are manipulating your brothers?"

"Well no. They are great women."

"Then what is your explanation for not trusting women again?" she asked, shoving her fingers through her bedhead hair, trying to straighten it out.

"I told you about Loren."

"Yeah, so?"

"It's difficult trusting someone with your heart when you've been stepped on like that. I see the way my parents are with each other, and I want a relationship like that. I want to be with my special someone for the rest of my life. I want what my brothers have. I want to come home to my wife every night after work, kiss her on the lips and have her melt in my arms the way my mother does when Dad kisses her. They've been married a long time, and they still can't get enough of each other." He grabbed her by the upper arms. "Don't you want it too?"

"Yes." *With you.*

"Then don't settle for less with anyone."

"I don't plan on it."

He leaned in, bringing their mouths close but not touching. "Why do I get the feeling when you walk away in a couple of weeks, I'll be losing something special?"

"Because you will be." She brushed her mouth against his in a tender kiss. "It's not the right time for us though. We both have too much going on to give up our lives as they are on the whim that this might be love."

"Might be?"

"Do you love me, Joshua?"

"I don't know."

"If you did, you'd know."

* * * *

He didn't like the look in her eyes. The sadness hurt his heart. Did he love her? He wasn't sure, and if anything she said was true, she might have feelings for him too. Could one fall in love in a few weeks? "I didn't mean anything by it."

"It's fine, Joshua. Things wouldn't work between us on a long-term basis. We've already come to this conclusion, so no worries." She smoothed her hands down her skirt. "I think we should get back to the house."

"Okay."

She didn't wait for him to open the door before she slid inside the cab of his truck, slamming the door behind her. He exhaled on a rush. He'd pissed her off, he figured by her attitude, although he wasn't sure what he'd done. Women. They sure were difficult creatures to deal with, and to love one seemed like insanity. Something kept him from falling for one, at least he figured he still was safe from the malady his brothers had. For now.

About twenty minutes later, he pulled into an empty spot in front of the big lodge house. The lights were on as usual, but something caught his attention through the dormer windows on the upper floor. A shadow passed in front of one, nothing solid, but something told him tonight would be a weird night from everything he'd experienced before.

"Listen. I think I'm going to take tomorrow for myself. You know, go shopping, read, or something."

"Okay." He frowned as he glanced up at the window again although nothing moved. "If you're sure. I need to get some things done around the ranch too. I have a saddle to finish for Terri's birthday. Jeff commissioned me to make it for her, and her birthday is in two weeks." He lifted her fingers to his lips for a quick kiss. "Come find me in my office if you want to go riding or something."

"I will." She pulled her hand back in a slow, reluctant stretch. "I'm sorry about tonight."

"Nothing for you to be sorry for. I screwed up."

"So we're both sorry, and we can move on from this discussion?"

"Sure."

"Good." She didn't move for a moment as she stared out into the darkness surrounding them. "How about if I get the kitchen to pack us a lunch and we go out by the pond tomorrow?"

"Sounds good. I should be able to take a break by then."

"Okay. I'll see you tomorrow at lunch then." She slid out of his truck and shut the door.

He watched her glance back for a second before she went inside and closed the door behind her. Why did he feel like shit giving her such a line of crap out in the woods? Yeah, he didn't trust women much, but he really did want a relationship with someone who would be his everything and his forever. He pressed his lips together as he looked at the steering wheel on his truck. He'd begun to think his feelings for Loren hadn't been real love. Yeah, he'd been hurt when she walked away from him to head off to New York, but it didn't compare to the feelings he was strongly beginning to think were love for Candace. Time wasn't something they had.

Anyway, tonight might be a good night for reflection and some deep thinking.

He pushed open the door on his truck, listening for any strange sounds before he shut the door behind him.

Children giggled in the distance. The ghosts were alive tonight with the full moon. They always seemed more active on the nights where the moon was the brightest.

Several minutes later, he walked up the stairs to his room. He paused a moment as he walked past Candace's door, wondering if he should knock. She'd become something special to him in the short time she'd been in Bandera, but he didn't think declaring his growing feelings would be the best move right now.

He twisted the keys to his truck around his fingers while he contemplated talking to her again this evening. Maybe giving her some space was a good thing. It seemed they both probably needed it after their love making tonight. He'd been balls deep inside her pussy, feeling like his heart would beat out of his chest. I love you hung on the tip of his tongue, but he swallowed it without uttering the words. He didn't want to be in love with her. She'd already told him Texas wasn't her thing. She had family and a business in California she would go back to in a week. He had to understand her life there came before him in any capacity.

With a heavy heart, he turned and headed for his room. The door stood open a crack as he approached, making him frown. *Who the hell has been in my room?* He walked inside and looked around. Nothing seemed out of place. His video games still sat in the entertainment center along with the console. His television still sat on top. His bed was made up neatly indicating his mother probably had been the one invading his space. She looked in his rooms sometimes, complaining at his lack of cleanliness.

The sweet smell of perfume reached his nose. His ghost lady was back.

He felt a soft touch on his arm as he turned toward the bathroom. A faint outline of a woman stood in the doorway. He'd never seen her before. This was new. Normally, he only felt her touch on his arm, his cheek or his chest and smelled her perfume.

"Joshua."

"You can't be here."

"I love you."

"You need to move on. You are dead."

"No."

"Yes."

A soft knock sounded on his door, and he watched as the ghost turned her head toward the sound.

"Joshua?"

A high pitched screech almost hurt his ears before the ghost quickly faded into the night.

"Joshua? Are you still up?"

"Yeah, hang on a minute." He moved toward the door and opened it to find his mother on the other side, leaning heavily on her crutches. "Mom? You shouldn't be doing the stairs on those. You'll hurt yourself."

"Hi." She frowned. "I know, but I needed to talk to you. What the hell was that sound?"

"I think we have a ghost problem."

"No shit."

"No really. There was a woman in my room by the bathroom. She was talking to me."

"Really?"

"Yeah. I think she's kind of hung up on me, and I'm not real comfortable with that."

"I bet. I can talk to the medium I know and see what her suggestion is. Sounds like we might need to see if we can get rid of her. Who is she?"

"I don't know. I think she might be a girl from the bordello days. Her outfit looked like a dancehall girl."

"I'll call my friend in the morning."

"Is there something else you needed, Mom?"

"I wanted to talk to you about a gift for your father for Christmas. How are you coming with the saddle you are making for him?"

"Good. It should be done in plenty of time." He glanced over her shoulder to where Candace's door stood closed.

"Are you okay, son?"

"Yeah."

"You seem preoccupied."

"I am a little, I guess."

She looked over her shoulder to where his gaze had landed. "Candace?"

"Yeah."

"She's a special young lady."

"That she is."

"Have you told her you love her yet?"

"What? No. I don't love her."

One eyebrow shot up over her left eye. "You could have fooled me."

"I can't love her, Mom. We haven't known each other very long."

"Love sometimes works like that, Joshua. Ask your brothers. Joel didn't know Mesa long. Jeff and Terri only knew each other a few short weeks. I could go on."

"I know, but I'm not like them."

She scoffed at that with a snorted laughter. "You think so?"

"What makes you think I love her?"

"The look in your eyes when you glanced over my shoulder to stare at her door. Does she love you?"

"She hasn't said she does."

"Women don't always say what is in their heart, son. Your brothers learned that the hard way."

"How did you know you were in love with Dad?"

She hobbled inside before he shut the door behind her. After he flipped on the light, he sat on the side of the bed to await his mother's words of wisdom.

"I just knew."

"That's it? Surely there is more to it than that."

"Nope."

"Well hells bells."

She laughed as she patted his knee. "You'll know, Joshua. If you can't think without her invading your thoughts, you're in love. If you want to be with her all the time and are miserable without her, you're in love. Do I think you can fall in love with someone in a few weeks? Sure, you can. You forget. You two have been together almost nonstop since you met. That has to mean something. Do you like her?"

"A lot."

"Have you two had sex?"

"Yeah."

"How was it?"

"Do I really want to have this conversation with my mother?"

"How was it?"

He hesitated a moment before he lowered his gaze to his knees. "She blew my mind."

"But that doesn't always mean love, now does it?"

"No. I've had good sex before, but this was different. It's like she touched my soul."

"Then I think you've got some serious thinking to do before she heads back to California."

"But she doesn't want to live here, Mom, and I can't see me living anywhere else. How do we overcome that kind of obstacle?"

"I'm not sure, honey. If she loves you and you love her, you'll work it out somehow. In the meantime, you should probably stay away from her. You know, so you two don't get more wrapped up in each other."

She kissed him on the cheek and left without another word.

His thoughts tumbled through his mind. Did he really love her? Yeah, maybe, he guessed. He raked his fingers through his hair, wishing he knew what he was supposed to think. This love thing sucked donkey balls. He didn't think he liked it very much. *Decisions, decisions. Now what the hell am I supposed to do?*

He flopped back on his head, staring at the ceiling. Love Candace. Okay. So he'd come to the conclusion that he might be in love with her, but what could he do about it? She didn't love him. He figured that much because she only wanted to experience everything cowboy.

Damn it! Why do I get myself in these messes? First Loren and now Candace?

Chapter Eleven

Morning sunlight came through the gauzy curtains on her window, blinding her to the room around her for a moment as she peeled her gritty eyelids open. She'd cried herself to sleep the night before, thinking about Joshua.

She'd stopped herself several times from going to his room, throwing herself into his arms and confessing her love for him. *Bad idea.*

After her tears had cleansed her soul, she'd drifted off to sleep with the taste of his kiss on her lips and the feel of his skin touching hers, if only in her dreams. She couldn't have him. She knew this. Their lives were too different and too far apart to come together even for love.

She'd decided to just enjoy the time they had together, never revealing the love growing in her soul for the cowboy in her life.

They would come together to enjoy her last week here, make love several more times, ride horses, go mudding again, and enjoy the stars and each other's company until she got on the plane for home, leaving her cowboy lover behind.

With a heavy sigh, she flipped the covers off her body, threw her legs over the side of the bed and sat up. She needed a shower to wipe away Joshua's love making from the night before so she could move on with her day. They would probably end up making love again out by the pond, but for now, she needed a clean slate to get this day started.

She'd found one of Mesa's books on the shelf downstairs a couple of days ago, and she wanted to read it before she went home. She might even go buy a copy at the bookstore in San Antonio to have her sign before she left.

She tapped her fingernails to her lips. San Antonio. Maybe she should make a trip into town this morning, do a little shopping, and get back before her lunch date with Joshua. Sounded like a plan to her. *I could buy some sexy little number to knock his socks off. Hmm.* Maybe one of the girls would go with her. She could always ask. Mesa? Paige? Peyton? She snapped her fingers. Mandy. She didn't have a brother she was hooked up with yet. She'd ask her after breakfast.

Smiling to herself, she grabbed some clean clothes and headed for the hot water of a shower.

Several minutes later, she whistled softly as she headed down the stairs to get some breakfast and ask Mandy to head into town with her.

When she rounded the bottom of the stairs, she almost ran headlong into Nina. "Oh, I'm sorry."

"I didn't see you." Nina hobbled back on her crutches, glancing over her thoroughly before she met her gaze again. "Don't you look gorgeous this morning?"

Candace looked at her attire, not really seeing what Nina referred to, but pleased all the same. "Thank you. It's nothing special."

"Maybe it's the twinkle in your eyes. You look beautiful."

"I appreciate you saying so. How are you today?"

"Wonderful! It's a beautiful day here on Thunder Ridge." She leaned in to whisper, "I have it on good authority, one of my boys is expecting a baby. I'm going to be a grandma again."

"Oh?"

"Yes, ma'am, but I've been sworn to secrecy. His spouse hasn't told him yet, so I have to keep it quiet." The smile on her face was big enough, Candace was afraid she was going to start giggling.

"Congrats," Candace whispered in conspiracy.

"Thank you."

She glanced over at the group sitting at the table as they laughed together. No one seemed worse for wear after their night at the bar. Her gaze went around the table to each of the women wondering who was pregnant this time, but she couldn't decide. No one looked anymore sickly or glowing or whatever the newest thing was to tell if a woman was pregnant. Maybe it was still very early, and she wasn't showing the signs yet. It would give her something to think about besides Joshua. "I'm heading into San Antonio this morning for a little shopping. Is there anything I can pick up for you?"

"No, but thank you for asking. I'll be making a trip myself in a couple of days for baby shopping. I do love it when my kids are having new babies." She grinned again, looking over her shoulder at her sons and daughters, but Candace couldn't tell who she was looking at.

"I believe I'll ask Mandy to go with me, if you don't mind."

"Oh no. I'm sure it would be fine, but she'll need to check with the head cook to find out if it's okay. I don't get involved in time off things."

"I'll have her ask then."

"Good." Nina turned her toward the breakfast serving area. "Go eat before you waste away."

"Not likely to happen in this lifetime."

"Oh psh."

Candace laughed. She really loved Joshua's mother a lot, and she hoped someday she would get another great daughter-in-law like the others she had. The thought of Joshua with another woman didn't sit well with Candace at all. She didn't want to wish him years of loneliness, but she sure as hell didn't want him with anyone else either.

When she walked toward the serving tables, she could feel a gaze on her. She hadn't seen Joshua at the table, but he was near. Wanting to give him something to think about while he worked, she swished her hips slightly as she walked. He like her butt, she knew that from their romping anal sex.

Holding out her plate for the servers to give her eggs, bacon, hash browns and a biscuit, she looked at Mandy and said, "Would you like to run into San Antonio with me today? Can you get off work?"

"Let me ask after we are done serving, and I'll let you know."

"Okay." She reached the end of the serving line, grabbed an orange juice and headed for a table at the end of the room. She fully expected Joshua to join her, but he didn't. She brought a forkful of eggs to her mouth, slipping the tines between her lips as she locked her gaze on him, sitting by himself at a side table away from the family.

One eyebrow shot up over his left eye while a small smile played on his lips, tilting the right edge up slightly in a cocking little grin.

We're playing like that, are we?

Once she swallowed, she slowly parted her lips, running her tongue over the bottom one in what she hoped was a sexy little move meant to drive him nuts. Seeing him shift in his chair, she wondered why he didn't come over.

While she continued to eat her breakfast, he stared, hardly blinking, his crystal, blue gaze fixated on her. Her nipples pebbled behind her bra, rubbing enticingly against the material, reminding her of his tongue rasping over the surface. Her pussy throbbed to the beat of her heart, nearly driving her insane with lust.

How could he wind her up like this without even touching her? The man had her so tightly wound, she could easily follow him out to his office, jump his on his desk, and never think twice about it.

She blinked when Mandy stepped between them, breaking their fixation on each other.

"I got the day off so we can go to San Antonio."

"Great."

"Are you okay? You look flush."

"I'm fine. Just a little warm is all."

Mandy glanced behind her to where Joshua sat grinning like a Cheshire cat who got the cream.

Bastard. For that, I'm not going to tell him I'm switching our ride to dinner time. Make him wonder until he finds the note I'm going to leave in his office.

"I'll be ready to go in a few minutes. I need to do something first."

"Okay. I'll help the kitchen do up a few dishes while I wait for you."

"Awesome. I'll meet you here in like ten minutes."

"I've got your plate. You go on and do your errand."

"Thanks, Mandy." Candace blew Joshua a kiss before the door banged shut behind her as she headed to his office. She wanted to get there and leave him a note about their outing.

She pushed open the office door, breathing in the scent of leather and man. The intoxicating smell made her want him all the more. After a moment, she shook her head to jar the titillating thoughts from her mind. *Focus, Candace.*

She found a pen and some paper on the desk to write a quick, sexy note.

> *Joshua-*
> *Sorry to change our lunch plans, but I thought this would be more fun.*
> *Meet me here at 8 p.m. dressed for a midnight ride with your fantasy cowgirl.*
> *~ Candace*

She pressed a lipstick kiss to the paper, giggling softly for a moment before she laid the sheet on the desk where he could find it.

Now to get Mandy's help with the cowgirl thing.

Smiling as she thought of Joshua finding the note, she snuck around the side of the barn when she spotted him across the yard heading toward his office. She hoped he had a hard-on all day long because she knew she was horny for him and would be until they met later that evening.

The moment he went inside, she dashed toward the main lodge to find Mandy.

Several minutes later found the two of them laughing as they drove down the driveway toward the wrought iron gates of Thunder Ridge, headed for San Antonio and a girl's day out.

The first store they hit was Ranch at the Rim, a western wear store with a huge selection of boots, dresses and things for the cowgirl in all of us. She found the perfect short black dress with long flowing sleeves and a silver concho belt to go with it. She already had new boots, but she found a solid black pair with inlaid turquoise and silver accents. They would go perfect with her dress and the turquoise jewelry she found at another western store. The earrings would dangle enticingly against her neck, drawing his gaze, making him want to nibble on the long expanse. The chunky necklace dangled a large group of turquoise beads near her breasts, with silver feathers and hearts going up the sides to clasp at the back of her neck.

She stood in front of the mirror at the final store with the entire outfit on.

"Wow. You look like a red-haired Indian princess," Mandy said, standing behind her. "Joshua won't know what to do with you. How are you going to ride in that though?"

"With it up around my waist, silly. And no underwear." She laughed.

"Ouch. I think that would chafe."

"I'll bring something to put on the saddle so it doesn't."

"Are you planning on seducing him right out of his tight Wranglers?"

"Hell yeah."

Mandy sighed happily.

"Who are you hung up on?"

"I'm not."

"Oh please. I can tell by the way you glance constantly at the family table, but I can't tell which one of those sexy guys has your attention."

"It doesn't matter. He doesn't know I exist."

"Who?"

Mandy glanced around for a minute before answering, "Jonathan."

Candace met her gaze in the mirror. "Oh, the website guy."

"Yeah."

"He's not your typical Young brother cowboy."

Mandy picked at her fingernails, not meeting Candace's gaze any longer. "No, he's not, but yeah, that's why I want him, I think. The other guys are gorgeous, don't get me wrong, but there is something about him that trips my trigger."

"What do we need to do to get him to notice you?"

"I don't know. I'm tired of chasing his ass."

"Sounds like love to me." She laughed a little as she thought about how her relationship with Joshua had gone in the few weeks she'd been at the ranch. Who had done the chasing? She wasn't sure anymore. It seemed mutual to her. Joshua hadn't chased her really. The accident with the beer had started the whole thing. Of course, he'd been happy to oblige, she was sure. He hadn't turned down her advances. Typical guy, really.

The dress swished around her thighs when she turned from side to side, admiring the way it clung to her curved waist and breasts. She liked the look and feel of the clingy material against her body. It made her feel sexy.

"You look great," Mandy said, admiring the reflection. "The dress looks fabulous on you. He'll be totally blown away."

"And the boots?"

"They are perfect for that dress too. You look like the quintessential cowgirl. Now all you need is a black hat. I'm sure this store has a few of those." Mandy laughed as they both looked at the rows and rows of cowboy hats lining the area to the right of the dressing room.

Different brands with everything from snakeskin headbands to feathers hanging down the back, lined the walls. She could have her pick. "I'm sure I can find one that looks good. Although I'm not sure if black looks better on me or brown with my red hair."

"The black looks fabulous on you. Your hair isn't a bright red, it's more of a strawberry blonde, so the black is perfect."

"Okay. Black it is then."

"Good choice."

"What shall we do for lunch?"

"There are some great little shops near the Alamo, and the River Walk is right there. They have some fantastic restaurants with everything from Tex-Mex to steak."

"Joshua hasn't really taken me anywhere except the ranch and The Dusty Boot."

"Well, he needs to then. These restaurants are really romantic. Some even have Mariachi bands that'll play for you specifically. For a price, of course."

"Of course."

Candace went back inside the dressing room to put on her jeans and blouse so they could head down to get some lunch. She wanted to shop for something special to give Joshua. She wanted him to remember her when she went back home. *Something special, but what?*

What do you buy for a man who has everything or seems to?

After she redressed, she stepped out into the main area of the western store only to run smack into Loren. "I'm sorry. I didn't mean to bump into you."

"Oh. It's fine." Loren glanced up at her from her small stature. "You're the woman who was with Joshua the other night."

"Loren, right?"

"Yes." Loren gave her an attempted intimidating look. "You realize he's mine, right? He'll never love anyone the way he loved me and still does."

Candace placed her hands on her hips. "If I understand correctly, you left him to run off to New York. What makes you think he'd take you back?"

"Because he still loves me, you idiot."

"Really, because I'm not getting that vibe from him. I think he's over you, and you don't like it because he's moved on with someone who will treat him like he's everything to them."

"And that's you?"

She hesitated a moment, realizing she wanted him to be her everything, but she couldn't. She had a life in Los Angeles, her family, and her business. "Whether it's me or not is none of your business. Obviously, it isn't you since you walked away from him without a backward glance. Why are you back in Bandera? Did your glamorous life in New York not work out?"

"You're a bitch."

"And you're one to talk. It takes one to know one, and by that I mean, yes, you are a bitch too. At least Joshua's feelings mean something to me. They apparently didn't to you when you walked away from him."

"I asked him to come with me."

"Did you? I doubt that, but anyway, how could you ask him to give up his life here? He's a cowboy. He would shrivel up and die in a place like New York." *Or Los Angeles.* She frowned.

"He didn't give a shit about my wants or needs either. My career took me to New York. If he loved me, he would have dropped everything to go with me."

"If you loved him, you wouldn't have asked."

"Well anyway, you can just go back to where you came from and leave him to me. I'm back in Bandera to stay. He'll be mine again soon."

"I doubt that."

"I don't. I saw the way he looked at me at the bar."

"Old feelings die a slow death, but give up, Loren, his feelings for you are dead."

"We'll see about that."

With a flip of her hair, Loren walked out of the store as Mandy and Candace looked at each other.

"Well that was entertaining." Mandy raised an eyebrow and smiled.

Candace laughed although her heart was heavy. The realization she was falling in love with Joshua hit hard, right between the eyes. She'd realized it before, but right now she could totally see him going back to Loren. It bothered her, a lot. Walking away from him came with a price. The price would be a broken heart. A heavy sigh escaped her lips as she headed to the checkout with her purchases. She would live for the moments they had together so she'd have something to hold onto when she went home. Her life in California came before what her heart wanted. Her head said walk away, you still have a life there with your family, friends, and business. He's just another guy. Her heart said no, he was the one. Stay and work it out, but she didn't know how to do that.

Lunch was a quiet affair after all their bantering back and forth in the western store. Mandy seemed quiet too. Thoughtful might be a better word. "Are you okay?"

"Yeah, why?"

"You're pretty quiet."

"Just thinking."

"About what?"

"What else. The Young brother who I can't seem to corner long enough to talk to me."

"We should brainstorm ideas on how to get you two together."

Mandy sighed as she plopped another chip dripping with salsa into her mouth. The moment she finished chewing, she said, "Trust me, it doesn't work. I've tried that with Peyton, Paige, Mesa, Terri and Callinda. They all have their men, but mine doesn't seem to notice anything outside of HTML codes and graphics."

"He's a Young brother, is he not? What about sex?"

"If I thought that would jingle his bells, I would be all over him. I'm beginning to think he might be gay, but I've seen him with a woman or two before, so I know that's not the case either. It's got to be me. He doesn't like blondes? My boobs are too big or too small? I'm too fat? Hell, I wish I knew."

"You are not too fat. You're curvy and just the right size for your height."

She blew out a breath, puffing her cheeks out in a heavy sigh. "Maybe that's it. Maybe I'm too short for him." The straw made a swishing sound when she stirred her margarita with it.

"Oh, stop."

"You can say that. You have a Young brother to yourself."

"Temporarily. We aren't anything permanent, you know. I have to go back to California next week."

"Why?"

"Why what?"

"What's in California that is so important to give up Joshua?"

Candace thought to herself for a moment before she said, "My family."

"They can come visit."

"My apartment."

"You could find something here. There are cheap apartments all over Bandera."

"My business."

"Sell it. Didn't you say your brother was your vice president? I bet he'd buy it in a heartbeat."

"What if I don't want to sell it?"

"Ever hear of relocating your business here? San Antonio is a hubbub of new business starting up all the time. Web design is huge here."

"I don't think Joshua is on the permanent relationship trail. We are having a good time together, but he hasn't said anything about making this a long-term relationship."

"Do you love him?"

Now it was her turn to stir her drink as she contemplated how to answer Mandy's question. Telling her the truth would bring about a flurry of Mandy trying to convince her to stay in Bandera. Her heart wanted her to, but her head said no. How could she possibly pull up her life and move here when she didn't even know if Joshua felt anything for her? Yeah, they were good in bed together, but a couple needed more than that to make a life together, and what happened if they didn't make it? What if she pulled up stakes, moved everything here, and then they broke up somewhere down the line? No, she would be better going back to California and forgetting the man ever existed. It was best. "I have feelings for him, yes, but I can't uproot my life when I don't know if there is anything there for him."

"Have you told him?"

"Hell no. Do I look stupid to you?"

"No, you don't. I think you're trying to protect your heart, and I can really understand that. I can, but if you don't take the chance, you will never know if there is a chance you could make a go of it."

"What if he laughs in my face?"

"I doubt Joshua would do that, but if you are that afraid, wait until you have him buck naked, take his clothes and don't give them back until he professes his love for you."

The laughter coming from her mouth burst out is a loud bubble of giggles and snorts until she covered her mouth and nose, afraid the drink of margarita she'd just taken might spew forth in a shot of alcohol across the table, hitting Mandy square in the face.

"I'm glad I could make you laugh. This conversation was getting a bit too serious." Mandy giggled in return.

"I needed that. Thank you."

"You're welcome." Mandy sobered. "Now, you need to tell him tonight when you have him alone under the stars. See what he says. What can it hurt?"

"I might lose my soul."

"Yeah, but what a way to go!"

"You're a nut!"

Mandy raised her hands as she shook them over her head. "Yep, that's me, nutty Mandy."

Their lunch arrived bringing their conversation to a halt while they dug into their respective plates. Candace enjoyed the tang of Mexican food on her tongue as she savored the spices blended together in her Texas Red Enchilada. While she ate, her thoughts wandered to Joshua as she debated on what to do about him. Yes, her feelings for him were growing stronger every day she was around him, but he never gave any indication her feelings might be returned. What if they were? Could she really pack up and leave her life in California for the love of a man who had trust issues? Would he ever be able to fully trust her after what Loren did to him?

"What are you thinking about?"

"Joshua."

"Big surprise." Mandy took the last bite of her taco salad before pushing her plate away. "Any conclusion?"

"Nope."

"I say play it by ear. If those three little words are on the tip of your tongue tonight as they dance along his cock, then say them. See what happens."

"You are such a bitch."

"I know." Mandy grinned before she swallowed the last of her drink and then leaned back in her chair. "Lordy, I ate too much."

"Me too," Candace replied, pushing her unfinished plate away. "We have more shopping to do though."

"Oh?"

"Yeah, I want to get something special for Joshua."

"Do you know what you are looking for?"

"No, not really. I'll know it when I see it though."

After they paid their bill, they headed out to check out the shops along the River Walk. She'd heard they had specialty shops there that carried all sorts of things a cowboy might want. It needed to be something special, something he couldn't get just anywhere.

When she was about to give up and buy him a hat, they walked down one more street of shops where a small leather tanner and craftsman's shop sat in the back in a tiny area with a glass front. The man had saddles, belts, hat bands, and several other things he'd worked some beautiful patterns into the leather with. She could imagine Joshua doing this full time. He would love it!

As she browsed around the shop for something special to give him, the gentleman looked up from his work and smiled. "Howdy."

"Good afternoon. Are you the owner of this shop?"

"Yes ma'am. Name is Michael West. What's yours?"

"Candace."

He glanced around his shop with a twinkle in his eyes. "Is there somethin' I can show you?"

"I'm not sure. I'm looking for something special to give a man I know. He does this kind of work too."

"Oh?"

"Yes. His name is Joshua Young."

He slapped his knee and laughed. "I know Joshua well. I taught him everything I knows."

"You do?"

"Yes ma'am. Nice boy. He's talented, that one. He's got some great stuff." Michael scratched his bearded cheek. "I haven't seen that boy in a long time. How's he doin'?"

"Wonderful. He's doing great."

"How can I help you?"

"I want to give him something special. Something he can't get anywhere else, but I don't know what. Most of this kind of thing, he can make for himself, you know what I mean?"

"Yes ma'am." He pushed his cowboy hat back on his head before staring her down with quizzical eyes. "I have just the thing."

"You do?"

"Yes'm." He moved to his desk to the right of where they stood and reached into a drawer. When he returned to her side, he held a leather bound square zippered pouched with JY on the cover. "I meant to give this to him a long time ago, but I haven't had the chance to get out to his place."

"What is it?"

"My old leather tooling kit, but I put it in a special case for him."

"Oh my. I couldn't possibly take this."

"I want you to give it to him. It'll be something he surely doesn't have, and it would be a special gift from you and me, if you don't mind me piggyback ridin' your gift."

"Not at all, but are you sure?"

Michael took his hat off, scratching his head for a second before replacing the worn straw hat on his head. "Most assuredly, ma'am. This would mean the world to me if you would give it to him with my special thank you."

"If you're sure."

"I would appreciate it a whole lot. You must be a special girl to Joshua to want to give him a gift like this."

Her face turned a bright red as she felt the heat crawl up her neck and splash across her cheeks. "I don't know how special, but we've been spending a lot of time together over the last few weeks, and he's come to mean a lot to me."

"I'm sure you mean a lot to him too, missy."

"Thank you, Michael. What do I owe you for this? I should pay you something."

"If you just pay for the leather case, we'll call it even. It's twenty dollars."

"No, it has to be more than that. I'll give you a hundred."

"No, ma'am. Twenty is all."

"Twenty it is then." She handed him the twenty, fully intending to drop another hundred on the floor as she left so he would find it under his desk another time. When Michael turned to put the tool case in a bag for her, she slipped a hundred dollar bill into his desk drawer and turned back to face him. "Thank you, Michael. I'm sure he'll be thrilled with it."

"I'm sure he will. Tell him hello for me when you see him."

"I certainly will." She leaned in and gave him a smooch on the cheek. "Thank you again, and I hope to see you soon."

"Me too, sweetie."

Leaving the shop with Mandy, Candace held the bag close to her chest knowing what a special gift it was for Michael to give Joshua his tooling kit. It would mean the world to him to have his mentor's tools to work the leather with.

Evening fast approached. She wanted to take a shower, curl her hair, and put on her little black dress with her boots and jewelry before she met Joshua in his office and gave him his gift. Tonight would be special. She just knew it in her heart. Would she tell him she loved him? She wasn't sure, but for everything it was worth, she did love him. She just wasn't sure she could walk away from her life before Joshua to the possibility of life with Joshua.

Chapter Twelve

Joshua whistled softly as he worked with the belt he was making for Candace. He'd tooled her name into the back band of the leather, hoping she would like what he'd done with the flowers and such along the leather. He glanced down at the tool in his hand. *I need to get some new ones or sharpen these badly. They are pretty worn.* He shook his head when he remembered his mentor, Michael West. The man was a genius with leather, and Joshua only hoped one day to be able to work the designs that man could do in his sleep.

"Are you here?" Candace knocked on the closed door, calling through the panel.

He looked down at this watch before he shoved the belt into the desk drawer. "Yeah, hang on a minute, babe. I'll be right there." He didn't want her to see the belt before he was done with it, and he had a few more things to do to it before he gave it to her. Good thing she wasn't leaving until next week.

"Hi," he said, pulling open the door. His jaw about hit the floor at the picture she made. "Wow."

She twirled in a little circle, billowing out the edge of the dress that barely came to mid-thigh. "You like?"

"You look fabulous. Where did you get that dress and those boots?"

"Shopping today with Mandy. I had to have the perfect outfit for out little rendezvous tonight." She held out something in her palm.

"What's this?"

"A gift."

"You didn't have to get me anything, but that is very sweet of you." He unwrapped the leather binding and gasped. "A tool kit?"

"Yes."

"Where did you get this?" He ran his fingers over the initials on the back of the leather.

"A gentleman who had a shop in San Antonio. He said he knew you well. Michael West?"

"Seriously? He's my mentor. He taught me everything about tooling leather. You met him? What did he say?"

"Slow down, cowboy." She laughed. "He said you were one of the most talented people he knew, he enjoyed teaching you about leather, and how to work with it. When I told him I wanted to buy you a gift, he insisted on giving me this to give to you."

"Wow," he whispered. This meant more to him than anything in the world. "Thank you." He leaned in a kissed her. "You have no idea how much this means to me."

"I hope you like it."

"I love it! I'll probably spend all day tomorrow sharpening them."

She laughed as he turned to lay the kit on his desk, before he turned back around to take her in. She was definitely something special. When he stepped closer again, he slipped a hand up her thigh under the edge of her dress until he reached where her panties should have rested on her hip. "No underwear?"

"Nope. All yours."

"Holy shit," he whispered in awe of her boldness to go horseback riding with no underwear and bare legs. "Are you sure you want to ride like that?"

"I brought a towel to put on the saddle to keep the chafing down. I don't want to be rubbed raw before we get to the fun stuff."

He adjusted his cock in his jeans before groaning softly. "Me either, baby girl. Of course, it's going to be a bitch riding with the hard-on I have already seeing you like this." He watched her nipples bead under the soft fabric of the dress. "No bra either?"

"Nope."

"Damn," he whispered in awe. "Shall we? I've already saddled the horses unless you would rather ride double. My gelding can handle the weight if you'd rather ride across my lap."

"Now, that sounds like fun."

"Good." He pulled the door shut behind him and led her out into the walkway of the barn where the two horses stood. He quickly unsaddled the mare he'd prepared for her to ride, leading the horse back into an empty stall as soon as he finished.

He couldn't help but smile at her attire. The little black dress had long, flowing sleeves that hung to her wrists, with a square bodice and clingy material that hugged every curve of her body. There were small ruffles at the hem that went all the way around, but the most amazing thing to him was her legs. She had gorgeous, long legs he hoped to have wrapped around his waist before the end of the night. The boots on her feet were cute. Pointed toes with turquoise blue coloring woven into the design of the black boots were perfect for her outfit. The necklace around her throat showed off her long, slender neck to perfection, making his mouth water to taste her skin and drink in the beautiful woman she was, with everything inside him.

When he walked back to her side, he leaned in, capturing her mouth in a passionate kiss.

"What was that for?"

"Because you look gorgeous, and I couldn't keep myself from kissing you."

"Well, thank you, sir."

"You are most welcome, darlin'." She rubbed her arms. "Cold?"

"No. You call me darlin', and it gives me goose bumps."

He nuzzled her ear as he whispered, "Good. I like giving you goose bumps." After he stepped back a few inches, he positioned the towel she'd brought over the pommel before he grabbed her around the waist and deposited her into the saddle sideways so her legs hung off the left side of the horse. A moment later, he grabbed the saddle horn, stuck his foot into the stirrup and swung his leg over the back of the horse to settle himself comfortably into the saddle with her sitting across his lap. He made sure he sat back a bit in the saddle giving her a little room between him and the pommel. "Comfortable?"

"Yeah, actually, surprisingly enough, this isn't too bad."

"You'd better wait to make your decision. It might not be too comfortable when we start moving, but then again, you can always straddle me." *Stupid idea. Then her bare pussy would be riding my groin.*

"Oh, straddling you sounds awesome. I like that idea."

Kicking himself mentally, he lifted her by the waist until she swung one leg to his left and the other to his right, leaving her hot little pussy right against his dick. "Fuck."

"Uh-huh. Maybe I'll unzip you."

"I'm already going to die doing this. I need to keep my dick in my pants, little lady."

She stuck out her bottom lip in a little pout that he wanted to bite so badly, he hurt, or was it caused by her pussy scorching him through his pants? He might just die before they even got out of the barn.

With a blanket tucked behind him on the saddle, they were ready for their moonlight ride out to the pond. Good thing it wasn't too far away, and he wouldn't have to wait very long to be inside her. At least, he hoped not. At this rate, he didn't know if his legs would even hold him when he had the chance to stand again.

Moonlight streamed through the trees as they rode through some clearings toward the gurgling sound of the stream running through Thunder Ridge property. He loved coming down here. It had always been a special place for him, and now it would be a special place for them. A place they could look back on and remember fondly about how they spent the evening making love under the stars, with the moonlight shining down on them in a curtain of silver. Tonight was the back half of the full moon from the night before. Something special. He just knew it in his heart.

They reached the pond with the babbling brook running over the rocks, producing the soothing gurgling sound they'd been hearing for the last several minutes.

He groaned softly as he disengaged himself from Candace's lips where she'd been kissing, licking, and sucking on his neck for half the ride.

"Oh. Are we here?"

"Yeah."

"Good, but I was having fun."

"I know you were. You were torturing me beyond belief while I had to keep the horse on the damned trail."

"Poor cowboy." She trailed her fingers down his erection. "A little hard, are we?"

"A lot hard, babe." After he disengaged her legs from around his waist, he swung his leg over the saddle and stood on shaky legs when his booted foot hit the ground. "My legs feel like I haven't ridden in a years."

He put his hands around her waist and helped her to stand beside him. With her hands on his shoulders, she brought their lips together in a heart stopping kiss meant to melt him into a puddle, he was sure.

"Mmm. I can't wait to get these jeans off you, cowboy."

"I brought some dessert in the saddle bags along with a blanket."

"Good thinking. Chocolate, I hope?"

"Yeah, chocolate cake from dinner. I hope it's in one piece."

"Licking the crumbs from your chest would be fun. Too bad we don't have chocolate syrup."

He reached into the bag and pulled out a bottle.

"Awesome! You think of everything, don't you?"

"I try." He grabbed the blanket and handed it to her. "Why don't you find a nice grassy spot while I hobble the horse? I'll join you in a minute."

He watched as she walked over to the stream, found the perfect spot, rolled out the blanket and sat down. Mesmerizing was the word that came to mind before he shook his head to dispel the kinky thoughts running through his brain so he could tie the horse. He wanted her with every breath in his body, every ache in his dick, and every droplet of sweat pouring down his back on the ride over here. The perfection that was Candace wound its way around his soul. *I am so screwed.*

* * * *

Candace sat on the blanket and removed her boots. With her toes now free, she wiggled them a bit to get the cramps out of them from the pointed toe boots. She loved how they looked on her feet, but being comfortable in them wasn't great. Maybe she needed to stretch them out some before she wore them again. She loved that Joshua liked her outfit though. She'd done everything for him.

A few moments later, he slid down beside her on the blanket, half his face in the shadows from the moonlight and the other half lit brightly by the silver lighting. She could still see the twinkle of desire in his eyes, and boy howdy, she couldn't wait to get him naked. She had plans for his body tonight, some she hoped he wouldn't mind because she wanted to ride his hips into next week. "Are you going to take your boots off?"

"Yep. I see you've already got comfortable."

"Yeah. I love the boots, but they pinch my toes a little."

"You need to stretch them out. You should probably take them to a cobbler and have them stretched for you a little, but just wearing them a lot will help."

She smiled at his ever helpful attitude. He always wanted to help someone. It was his nature. "Thanks."

After he yanked his boots and socks off, he put them to the side of the blanket and lay back with his hands behind his head. All she wanted to do was curl up next to him, lay her head on his chest and stay that way forever. Tonight would have to do.

She curled up next to him, put her head on his chest and tucked into his body. "This is nice."

"I like holding you like this."

"It's perfect."

Quiet surrounded them except for the crickets, frogs, birds, and other nighttime animals making their sounds. She didn't mind though. It almost sounded like a chorus of noise meant to soothe someone. She laughed as she thought about how noisy it really was.

"What's so funny?"

"The noises. It would almost be quiet if not for all the sounds."

A laugh rumbled in his chest, reverberating in her ear. "I know what you mean. It gets pretty noisy with all the animals."

She lifted her head, looking up into his eyes. "Kiss me, cowboy."

"My pleasure, darlin'."

He lifted up, rolled her onto her back, leaned in and took her lips. His right hand wandered down to cup her breast while he devoured her mouth with his. *Good God.* She loved kissing this man more than anything on earth. Well, maybe not anything. She liked making love with him more.

His right hand inched down from her breast to the ruffled edge of her dress to slowly pull it up until she left the warm summer breeze against her wet pussy. Why she was surprised she was wet for him already, she wasn't sure. Being around this man had her wound up tighter than a spring from the moment they'd met.

He kissed his way from her lips to her ear, tonguing the lobe for a moment before he captured it between his teeth. The sensation sent goose bumps flittering across her skin from her head to her toes.

"I love the way you smell, all subtle right here behind your ear, along your neck, and down between your breasts."

His lips followed the path he described until he reached the edge of her dress that lay along her breasts. The tip of his tongue traced little swirls along her skin. Her nipples pebbled when he pushed the material farther down, but not quite low enough to reach the peaking flesh. His hand snaked up her thigh until he could skim it across her abdomen. Her belly jumped at his touch.

"Your skin is amazingly soft."

She moaned as his fingers danced along her lower belly, barely touching. "Touch me. I need you."

"Oh, I plan to."

"You're teasing me."

"Yep. Anticipation is half the fun."

He worked the top of her dress down over one breast, taking the stiff peak between his lips in a strong suck. She arched her back, pushing the flesh deeper into his mouth. After she tossed his hat the side, she threaded her fingers through his hair, holding his head against her breast.

Her thigh spread of their own accord, in a silent beg for him to touch her. His hand strayed down between her thighs. She sighed when his fingers finally pushed between her pussy lips to glance across her clit.

"Yes."

He released her breast, kissing his way to the other one as he pushed a finger into her pussy. "You are so wet."

"Only for you. I've never been this wet before with anyone else."

"Ah, flattery will get you anything you want, darlin'."

"Anything?" She took a deep breath and blurted out, "Your heart?"

His movements stopped when he paused in mid-stroke.

"Sorry. I didn't really mean it the way it sounded."

He lifted his head, staring down into her face. His face was bathed in silver light from the moon overhead, his eyes glittering with something she wasn't sure she wanted to name. Without saying a word, he returned to his assault on her senses. She released a pent up breath. She didn't want him to say anything, really, afraid he would either deny her growing feelings or affirm them in a way she wasn't ready for. *Damn traitorous heart anyway.*

After several minutes of getting her worked up enough, she was ready to beg for him to make love to her. He sat up and removed his jeans and shirt, revealing the magnificent form of Joshua Young to her gaze. The springy hair on his chest tickled her breasts when he came back to lay over her form.

"Do I need a condom?"

"No."

He slowly pushed all of his hard flesh between her pussy lips until he was fully inside her body. With her legs wrapped around his hips, holding his pelvis against hers, she hoped to keep him close for just a few minutes longer.

"I've got to move, darlin'. I'm about to explode being inside you like this."

"No eight second ride, please."

"Not on your life, but I'm not sure how long I'll last. You are burning me alive with your hot pussy."

"Fuck me, Joshua. Give it all to me. I want to feel every inch of you inside me."

"You got it, babe."

He slowly started their mutual climb to explosive satisfaction with his measured movements. Her body sang with each stroke. Her pussy quivered with need, hovering on the edge of insanity as she reached the pinnacle of a climax and held there waiting for him.

"Come with me, Candy. I need your sweetness."

It was the first time he'd called her by her nickname. Her body reacted to his deep thrust by pushing her into the most explosive climax she'd ever had. Her world detonated into a kaleidoscope of color behind her eyelids as she screamed his name at the top of her lungs. Bird flew from the trees around them. Frogs stopped croaking. The only sound was his harsh breathing in her ear and the gurgling of the water nearby.

After several minutes, he shifted his weight onto his elbows and looked down into her face. "You okay?"

"Perfect."

He smiled, his teeth flashing white in the moonlight. "Glad I could take care of you."

"You always do."

"I try."

"You succeeded beautifully."

He brushed his lips over her eyelids before reaching her mouth for a drugging kiss. "We should probably head back."

She wrapped her hands around his back, holding him close. "Not yet."

"I could stay like this forever."

"Me too."

They both groaned as he removed his softening cock from her core so he could shift over to her side. Lying beside him like this was a dream come true. He stroked her hair back from her face as he gazed down into her eyes. She couldn't read him though. "What are you thinking about?"

"You and how beautiful you are lying here in the moonlight."

She smiled as a little harsh laugh escaped her mouth. "No, really?"

"Really."

"Hmm."

"What about you? What are you thinking about?"

"How sticky my legs feel."

He laughed as he sat up and reached for his shirt. "I suppose we should be gettin' back to the house."

"Yeah, I guess."

She sat up, pulling her dress back into place to cover her nakedness as she shook her head. In the rush to copulate, they missed the cake and chocolate syrup all together. What does that say about her? Embarrassment flooded her cheeks. Thankful for the darkness of the night, she put her boots on before heading to where the horse stood hobbled.

"Are you all right? You're awfully quiet."

"Yeah, I'm fine."

"You don't sound fine."

She bit her bottom lip and fixed her gaze on the tips of her boots. He put two fingers under her chin to raise her gaze back to his.

"What is it?"

"I feel like such a slut."

"A slut? Why?"

"We didn't even get my dress off before fucking on the ground. What does that say about me?"

"You aren't a slut, Candace. We wanted each other. There is nothing wrong with that."

"Yes, I understand the need part, Joshua, but couldn't we have at least got my dress all the way off?"

He pushed his hands into her hair, cradling her head with his palms. "I thought it was sexy how you couldn't wait for me to pleasure you."

"Really?"

"Yes, really. It says you are a woman who takes what she wants and doesn't worry about what others think. You are sexy as hell, and I couldn't wait to have you." He kissed her lips lightly before continuing. "In fact, every time we've been together, I haven't been able to wait to have you. It says you are something special to me. I've enjoyed this time with you, and I wouldn't trade it for anything."

"Me either," she whispered, choking a little on the sentiment he'd just shared.

"I'm going to miss you when you go home."

"I'll miss you too. Maybe you can come visit me in Anaheim sometime."

"Maybe."

She sniffed a little and stepped back. "We should be getting back."

"Yeah." He stepped around her to cinch the saddle tight again while she grabbed the blanket to fold up.

Within a few minutes, they were both in the saddle, picking their way back toward the house. Conversation was minimal between them as she lost herself in thought. She would be going home soon, a few short days away after being there for a few weeks. Her whole world had changed with one spill of a beer down the back of his shirt. How would she function without him around when she went home? She wasn't sure, but she would have to. Yes, she wanted to be more than a mere roll in the hay to him. She didn't think that was possible. He might care for her a little, she guessed. Not enough to build a relationship on and really, she wasn't prepared to leave her life in California for Texas.

The cowgirl way of life seemed fun to play at for a while, but she missed her office, her employees, her family, and the milder weather of California. Hot, steamy Texas didn't suit her needs at all. Besides, what really would she have here?

It's not like Joshua had professed his love for her with a ring and a proposal.

Chapter Thirteen

Last night, after they'd went to their own rooms, Candace had spent a lot of time thinking about what she wanted from her relationship with Joshua. She wanted him more than anything, so she decided to talk to him about her feelings and see where they might lead.

The more she'd thought about it, the more she'd decided she might be willing to see how things went. They could try a long distance relationship. It wasn't like she couldn't afford to fly out here every few months to see him and maybe pay for him to fly out to Los Angeles to see her. Surely, he could take some time off at the ranch to be with her too, right?

She walked into the barn headed for his office to see if he wanted to spend some time talking, just the two of them.

He meant a lot to her, but she wasn't sure it was love. Was it? She didn't know. She'd thought she'd loved before and things didn't work out very well with her ex. Was this love? Did she really love Joshua or did she just love the cowboy thing a little too much.

After a moment of knocking, she grabbed the handle to push open the door. He wasn't around that she could tell and hadn't been there this morning apparently. Stuff lay scattered on his desk, seemingly out of sorts with the person she thought he was.

Those familiar smells surrounded her. Leather, musk and Joshua swarmed her senses as she glanced from project to project around his space. She loved having this time to absorb him without him really being there. It gave her a sense of finding out more about him without him knowing.

She touched a few pieces of leather he'd been working on, hoping to bring a little of him into her soul while she contemplated how to handle their budding relationship.

A note of paper on the desk and the pen sitting on top of it didn't catch her eye, but the writing on the sheet did. It was her name in his expressive scrawl. Tears welled up in her eyes when she saw what he'd attached to it.

He'd written *Candace Young.*

Her heart tripped over itself in a hard gallop around her chest. *What the hell does that mean? Marriage? I thought he wasn't ready for that, and I know I'm not.*

Panic set in, bone chilling, mind numbing panic. She wasn't ready for this. He wasn't ready for this. He'd only barely gotten over Loren, right? He wasn't ready for marriage. She wasn't ready for marriage. She liked him, yeah, a lot, but this?

She needed to leave. She couldn't stay here any longer. If she broke his heart, she would never forgive herself, but living in Texas wasn't in her plans for her future and neither was a cowboy in a forever kind of basis. Yeah, she'd come to the realization she was in love with him, but it would never work. He needed to find his kind of woman, a cowgirl, who knew her way around horses, cattle, ranch work, and Texas. That wasn't her. She needed her parties, slinky black dress, high heels, and hairdressers, not cowboy boots, jeans, ponytails and no makeup.

After leaving his office in a rush, she headed to the house, but not before dashing behind a bush as Joshua came out, walking swiftly her way. *When had things gotten completely out of control? Shit. This is bad.*

The moment he was out of sight, she ran for the door. Home. She needed to go home and forget about all this cowboy stuff, this way of life and Joshua. Yeah, she needed to forget all about Joshua.

After a quick dash up the stairs, she rushed around her room throwing her clothes in the suitcase. She didn't even care if they charged her for the remaining days she was supposed to be there, she just knew she had to go and go now before things got worse.

With her suitcase in hand, she stopped at Nina's office. "Hey, Nina. Listen, I have family emergency in Los Angeles. I have to catch the next plane back, so I'm checking out."

"Is everything okay? You look worried."

"I am. It's my father, I mean my sister. Yeah, she's been in a car accident, and I need to be there for my parents."

"Oh, my. Of course, honey. You should go home to be with your family." Nina hugged her for a moment and then stepped back. The cast on her leg had been replaced by a walking cast so she wouldn't have to hobble around on crutches anymore. "Have you talked to Joshua?"

"No, I don't have time. The next plane leaves in three hours from San Antonio, and I have to return my car and everything. Can you tell him I'm sorry?" A tear slipped down her cheek as she wiped it away angrily. She didn't have time to cry. She could do that in the privacy of the car on the way to the airport, on the plane to Los Angeles or when she got home. Now, wasn't the time. "I'm so sorry, but he needs to find the right girl, and I'm not her."

"Are you sure you don't want to talk to him before you rush off? I know he's in the barn. I can go get him." Nina stepped around her, but stopped when Candace grabbed her hard with a cry of no.

"I'm sorry, but no. Thank you. You're always so worried about your boys, aren't you?"

"Of course, I am. I want to see them happy."

"Me too, Nina. That's all I want for him is for him to be happy."

"Why are you really running away, Candace?" Nina took her hands, forcing her to sit in the chair. "Are you in love with my son?"

"Yes, but I'm not the girl for him. He needs a girl from here. A cowgirl. A Texas girl, not me."

"I think he's in love with you, Candace. Why don't you give him a chance?"

"I need to go. Please, just let me go."

"Okay, honey. I don't want to pressure you. You have to come to terms with your love for Joshua by yourself and realize you two are meant to be together here in Texas."

She shook her head as tears streamed down her cheeks. "I can't. I won't give up my life for any man." She jumped to her feet before rushing out to her car, as she frantically pushed the button to unlock the door. If Joshua saw her or if she saw him, it would be all over but the singing.

* * * *

Joshua came out of the barn just as Candace was getting in her car with her suitcase. *What the hell?* "Candace?"

She shook her head, not meeting his gaze through the windshield. He walked toward her, but she jammed the car into reverse, spraying gravel and dust everywhere when she gunned the car.

He stood in stunned silence while she sped toward the iron gates of the ranch, punched the button to get out, and then squealed tires, trying to get away.

With his hands on his hips, he dropped his gaze to his boots. Somehow, he knew he would never see her again. It was over. Whatever they had, that is. Hell, he didn't know what they had, but apparently it scared the shit out of her so much, she ran, heading back home without a backward glance in his direction.

A moment later, he felt his mother's arms go around his waist as she put her head on his shoulder. "I'm sorry, Joshua."

"Me too, Mom. I only wish I knew what caused her to run?"

"I don't know either. I tried talking to her inside, but she wouldn't listen. She kept saying she wasn't the right girl for you."

"I think she is."

"So do I, honey, but until she comes to the same conclusion, it's a waste of time to pressure her. She needs space and going back to Anaheim will give her that space."

He sighed in a dejected exhalation. Loving a woman who didn't love you in return seemed to be the way his life would be forever. First Loren, now Candace. Would he never learn? "I'm done with women."

"You don't mean that, Joshua. Candace is scared, honey. Give her some time."

"Nope. I'm done. Getting laid is all I'm about anymore."

"You're hurt. I understand, but don't do something silly."

"I'm not. I'm living my life."

He walked back to his office with more purpose than he'd had in some time. He would live his life as a bachelor, sleeping with random women when he had the itch and never get involved with another one again.

When he stopped at his desk, he saw the pen and paper sitting there with his handwriting all over it. Why had he thought Candace might be different? What made him think she might love him in return and want to stay in Texas with him? With the tip of his finger, he traced where he'd written Candace Young. *Stupid.* He crumpled the paper in a wad and threw it across his office, bouncing it off the wall where the belt he'd been making for her hung by the fancy silver belt buckle he'd bought. He'd been almost finished with it, and he'd planned to give it to her today when they would go out for lunch. He moved toward it, taking the leather in his hands as he traced where he'd carved her name in the back of the belt. *What a fool I am to fall in love with a city girl.*

His cell phone jingled. When he picked it up, he realized he'd hoped it was her, but when Loren popped up on the caller ID, he debated on whether to answer it or not. She'd been decent in bed. Maybe he could get together with her for a quick fling and be done with her too.

"Yeah?" he answered the phone on the fourth ring.

"Joshua?"

"Yeah, Loren. It's me. What do you want?"

"I thought we could get together for coffee or something. You know, for old times' sake."

"Sure. When?"

"This afternoon at your aunt's diner?"

"How about in say fifteen minutes?"

"Sounds fine. I'll see you there."

* * * *

A short time later, he drove through town, headed toward his aunt's diner to meet Loren. He didn't really want to have anything to do with her, he'd concluded, but he had to do something to get over this sense of loss with Candace running away. He still couldn't believe she'd taken off without even talking to him. Why? He didn't know, and he'd tried to convince himself he didn't care. The hole in his heart told him different.

Why am I meeting Loren then?

He pulled into an empty space in front of the diner, shut the truck off and waited for a moment. Maybe he needed this to be able to really walk away from Loren, more than he needed it to come to some conclusion about Candace.

With a heavy sigh, he pushed open the door to the truck and then slammed it shut behind him. It was now or never. He needed to get this over with.

He walked inside the cooler interior of the diner, the door jingling behind him. The place was mostly empty except for Loren, sitting in a corner booth with a glass of Coke in front of her. He moved toward her as her gaze ricocheted up to meet his.

"Hi."

"Hi, Loren." He slipped into the booth on the opposite side from her.

"What can I get you, Joshua," his Aunt Anne asked, coming to the table.

"Coffee, please."

"Sure. Are you two planning on eating?" she asked, curiosity reflecting in her gaze bouncing back and forth between them.

"No. Just talking."

"Okay. Be right back."

He didn't start the conversation until after Anne had put the coffee in front of him and he'd doctored it the way he liked it. He needed to gather his thoughts before he told Loren to leave him alone. The spoon clanged as he stirred his coffee. He knew it irritated Loren to no end. He did it anyway.

She grabbed his hand to stop his movements. "Joshua, please. You know that bothers me."

"Yeah, I do." He set the spoon down on the table, took a sip of his coffee and then returned the cup to the table. "Why did you want to meet me, Loren?"

"I heard your little plaything took off back to Los Angeles this afternoon."

"News travels fast."

"I wanted you to know I'm here for you. You know I still love you, right?"

"No you don't, Loren. You want me because you can't have me. There is a name for that, you know. It's called being selfish. I realized while you were gone, you've always been that way. Whenever we were supposed to go somewhere, it had to be where you wanted to go. The food we ate had to be whatever you wanted to eat. The clothes I wore had to be what you wanted me to wear. I realized recently I didn't want to be in a relationship like that anymore, so I'm glad you decided to bail on us. Again, selfish on your part. It was all about what you wanted, not what we wanted as a couple."

"I'm not that person anymore, Joshua."

"It doesn't matter." He huffed out a laugh. "Something else I realized while I was with Candace. She liked me for me. She didn't try to change me and believe it or not, I love her." He looked around before coming back to face Loren again. "Yeah, I love her and by damn, I'm going after her because I love her, and I want her to love me in return. If she doesn't, that's okay because I can love her enough for both of us until she realizes she wants me too. I need her in my life, and I'm willing to go to whatever lengths it requires for her to be in my life."

He downed the coffee in his cup before pushing it away and getting to his feet. "Thank you for making me realize I needed to step up to the plate here and take what I want because it's the right thing to do." He grabbed a couple of dollars out of his pocket and tossed them on the table. "I hope you find what you are looking for, Loren. Just stay away from me from now on."

The door opened with a push of his hand. He had a woman to find and by damn, he planned to find her before she got on that plane.

After rushing home, he found his mom in the office and asked her what she knew about Candace's travel plans. His mom said she mentioned a plane leaving in three hours from the time she left the ranch. He glanced at his watch. That didn't give him much time. "Do you know which airline?"

His mom punched in a few things into the computer. "Yeah. Southwest is who she came in on. We require that information on the reservations for us, so

I'm assuming she's going home on the same airline."
She spun back around in her chair. "What are you going
to do?"

"Bring her home."

Nina grinned as she shooed him out the door.
"Don't forget flowers and a ring if you can."

"I don't have time for the ring, Mom, but flowers I
can do."

A moment later, he sent gravel flying behind him
as he took off for San Antonio airport to stop the
woman he loved from leaving him for good.

Driving up to the airport parking area, he glanced
at the clock. He didn't have much time to find her and
stop her from getting on that plane. He'd taken a few
minutes to stop at a local vendor for flowers before
hitting the airport. What he'd told him mom was the
truth. He needed a ring, but he didn't have time to buy
one. Candace would have to agree to go shopping with
him on the way home. Letting her leave on that plane to
Los Angeles wasn't an option as far as he was
concerned. He loved her. She had to love him too.

He skidded to a halt at the large sign announcing
the departures. He would have to figure out how to get
through security to get to the gate. Her plane was
leaving in thirty minutes. She was probably already
through security.

Coming up with a plan, he ran to the ticket counter.
Luckily, there was no line.

"Can I help you?"

"Yes, ma'am. I need to talk to a passenger on your
Los Angeles flight. Can you page her to come to the
ticket counter?"

"I can't do that, sir."

"Please?"

"It's against policy. Can you tell me what this is about?"

He went into a quick rundown of what was going on and a smile spread across the woman's face.

"How romantic."

"Thank you, but I really need you to help me out here. Maybe page her to tell her she left something at the ticket counter and she needs to return to claim it?"

"That might work, sir." The woman picked up the paging phone and spoke into the receiver. "Attention in the concourse, Los Angeles passenger Candace Alexander please return to the ticket counter to claim a lost item."

"Thank you. You have no idea how much this means to me."

"Just making her say yes to those beautiful flowers will be thank you enough." She shooed him with her hands. "If you stand in the corner over there, she won't see you until I direct her toward you."

Grinning, he nodded. "Thank you again."

"You're welcome."

The wait drug on until he finally saw her come rushing around the corner. She didn't seem to notice him approaching from his hidden spot either.

"I was paged to return to the ticket counter?"

"I'm sorry, ma'am, but we didn't page you."

"I heard it. It said there was a lost item here I needed to claim. I swear. I'm not lying."

"Candace?" He stood behind her with the flowers in hand.

She spun around, her eyes wide. "Joshua. What are you doing here?"

"I'm the lost item."

"Huh?"

"You need to claim me, darlin'. I can't live without you. I love you, Candace. Don't go back to Anaheim or if you have to, take me with you."

"I don't understand," she whispered in awe.

"I love you." He handed her the flowers and got down on one knee. The crowd around them hushed and the world seemed to stop spinning. "Marry me."

"You want to marry me?"

"Yeah, say yes."

"But, what about my life, my family, my business?"

"If you want to live in California, we will. I'll go with you. Just say you'll stay with me and love me forever. I don't want to be without you."

Tears streamed down her cheeks. "You love me enough to leave everything behind here in Texas and go with me to California?"

"Yes."

She pressed her fingers to her lips. "I love you too."

"Say you'll marry me."

"Yes. Yes, I'll marry you."

The crowd erupted in cheers as he stood and wrapped his arms around her. Lifting her, he twirled her around in circles, and enthusiastic applause broke out. They laughed together before he kissed her with all the pent up desire he couldn't express.

"You'll come home with me?"

"For now. We'll have to work out the arrangements somehow. All that matters is we love each other. The rest will work itself out."

"Perfect."

Once the airline managed to retrieve her bag before it was sent off to Los Angeles on the plane, he picked her up and carried her out to where his truck sat crooked between three parking spots. He hadn't had time to park correctly in the mad rush to get to her.

After she opened the door to his truck, he set her on the seat and kissed her directly on the mouth. "I love you."

"I love you too."

"Mom is going to be happy you said yes."

"You talked to Nina?"

"Yeah, she told me which airline to look for. Sorry for making you come back to the ticket counter. I couldn't think of any other way to get to you. The counter agent was a gem in her help."

"I couldn't think of what the heck I'd left at the ticket counter, but it was you. I was leaving you behind, and I realized I wasn't okay with that. You mean the world to me, Joshua." She frowned as she touched his face lightly. "What about Loren?"

"I'm done with her. We talked at the diner a little while ago, and she's the one who made me realize I couldn't let you go no matter what."

"Really?"

"Yeah. I knew my relationship with her wasn't a healthy one, but with you, it was so different. You get me. We're good together and you mean a hundred times more to me than she ever did." He rubbed his finger for her left ring finger. "We'll stop here at the mall and get you a ring, if you want to. I want everyone to know you're mine."

"If you'd like. I'm not in a rush. I know I'm yours. No one else matters."

"True." He kissed her again. "We'll wait then so you can pick out the perfect one."

"I need to call my parents."

"Okay. You can call them while we're driving back to the ranch. You'll be sleeping in my bed tonight."

One eyebrow rose. "Yeah?"

"You don't have a room anymore, and the inn is full." She grinned as he waggled his eyebrows at her.

"I can't wait."

"Me either." He shut the door on the truck before going around to the driver's side. "When do you want to get married?"

"I don't know. Give me a bit to absorb this. My parents are going to flip."

"Why? Won't they like me?"

"They'll love you, but it's going to be a shock. I wasn't even dating anyone before I left." She took his hand in hers. "I love you. That's all that matters."

"I'll never get tired of hearing that."

"Me either, so you better say it often, cowboy."

"Every day at least once."

"Good."

The one-sided conversation seemed to go well while he drove back to the ranch. She smiled a lot and seemed to be talking very happily with her parents on the phone. One frown did pop up on her face. He wasn't sure what they asked, but he figured it had something to do with money. He didn't have a lot of money like Jeremiah, but he had a nice savings account himself. They didn't have to worry. He didn't care how much money she had or didn't have. Money didn't mean much to him as long as they were happy.

"No, Daddy. I love him very much, and we're going to get married." She paused. "You'll get to meet him soon. I'm sure we'll come up there in the next few weeks so you can meet him."

He pulled her hand in for a kiss to the back.

"Okay. Two weeks from today? I'll make plane reservations when I get back to the ranch." She tipped her head to him with a silent okay?

He nodded as nervousness rushed through him. Meeting her parents gave him a stomachache. He hoped they wouldn't be difficult about the money thing. They would have to have a nice little chat after she was off the phone with them. He wanted to make sure she knew her money didn't mean anything to him.

"I love you, Daddy. Tell Mom bye. We'll see you in a couple of weeks. I'll text you our arrival time. Bye." She finally pressed end with a heavy sigh. "That went well."

"It didn't sound like it."

"They're worried, Joshua. I mean this kind of sprang up without warning, you know? We've only known each other for a few weeks and here we are getting married?"

"Are you having second thoughts about your feelings for me?"

"No. I know what I want. It's you, but you know how parents are. They tend to be cautious and mine are overly so. They know about my ex wanting me for the name and money. I'm sure they are thinking you are the same since we haven't known each other long."

"I don't care about your money, Candy. I have some of my own, although it isn't as much as your trust fund. You can keep your money. I'll sign a prenup if they want me to. I don't mind. Your money means nothing to me."

She unhooked her seatbelt before sliding over to rebuckle herself into the center seat. "Good to know, Joshua. I'm not worried."

"I have enough for us. If you want to work, you can. If you don't, that's okay too. I can get Jeremiah to help me invest so I can build my savings more. I wanted to do that anyway. He's a wiz at the financial stuff. He's managed to make a pretty little nest egg for my parents and himself. I'm sure he'd be happy to help us."

They pulled into the driveway at Thunder Ridge. While they waited for the gates to open, she turned to him and captured his mouth in a toe-curling kiss. "I love you. I don't care how much money you have or don't have. My money is our money." She kissed him again. "I've been thinking about selling my business anyway. I think my brother would buy it from me. Then my parents can't say anything because it's my money."

He pushed his hands into her hair. "Baby, it doesn't matter. It would be your money. We wouldn't have to touch it. We can live on my salary at the ranch and my savings. What's mine is yours."

"And what's mine is yours, Joshua."

They drove down the long driveway to be met by his mother standing on the walk waiting for them. "So?" she asked when they stepped out of the truck. "I'll assume this is good since she came back with you?"

"She's agreed to marry me."

Nina squealed as she hugged Candace in a big hug. "Welcome to the family!"

Epilogue

Joshua stood at the bottom of the stairs, looking over the group at the table. "Are you coming, Jackson?"

"Chill. I'm almost done. I'll meet you two outside."

"Fine, but we need to get moving. The concert starts in three hours. It's an hour drive to San Antonio."

"I know how far it is, asswipe. I've lived here as long as you have, plus I've driven there plenty of times. We'll be fine."

"But we have backstage passes to meet her, and Candace wants to get there in plenty of time."

"We have lots of time. Ease up, man."

They were headed to a benefit concert Candace had helped plan for a local children's hospital in San Antonio. She loved doing charity work. Since she was working on selling her business to her brother, she needed something to do with her time.

Samantha Harris was a huge country music artist. She'd agreed to do the benefit with the urging of Candace and her contacts in the music industry. She'd done a lot of computer security systems for Samantha, as well as others in the country music business. When Candy called her to do the concert, she jumped at the chance. Since Jackson liked country music, the two of them were dragging him to the concert so he could help with security for Samantha.

Joshua sighed when he thought about the meeting with Candy's parents and how well it had gone. They'd spent a couple of weeks closing up her apartment in Anaheim and getting a moving truck to bring her stuff to Bandera. Where they would put it all, he didn't know, but they'd figure it out once it all got there. She had a lot of stuff. Plenty to put a whole house together, and he hadn't even made plans to start building their house yet.

He glanced up the stairs when his fiancé descended to meet him at the bottom. He still couldn't believe how much he loved her or how lucky he'd been to find her when he'd been about as low as a human being could be when it came to love. "You look fabulous." Leaning in, he kissed her on the lips.

"It's nothing special. Just my cowgirl outfit."

He nudged her neck near her ear before dropping a well-placed kiss on that special spot he knew she liked so well. "I remember that outfit and the pond very well, thank you."

"Me too, cowboy." She left a little kiss on his cheek. "Are we ready?"

"Yeah, we're just waiting for Jackson, Mr. Head of Security."

"I'm coming, Geez!" Jackson got up from the table, placed his hat on his head and swept his hand wide, motioning for them to hurry up now.

Joshua and Candace followed him out to the truck. "I'm taking my own," Jackson announced. "I want to have my own vehicle."

"Fine. Do you know how to get there?"

"Of course, I do."

"Great. We'll see you there."

An hour later, they pulled into the Alamodome back parking lot where security was told to park. He and Candace stepped out of their truck while Jackson took up a spot next to them.

"Can I help you?" One of the security personnel, standing near two huge semi-tractor trailers with Samantha Harris' picture all over them, asked in a clipped tone.

"I'm Candace Alexander, this is my fiancé Joshua Young and his brother Jackson Young."

"Ah, yes. Ms. Harris told me you would be arriving soon. The command post for security has been set up to the left. Ms. Harris is on her bus near the back there. She said to send you right over, Ms. Alexander."

"Thank you. Jackson, I guess you need to check in with security so they can tell you where you need to be. I told them you were to be near Samantha at all times."

"Right." He saluted smartly before wandering over to the tent with his hands in his pockets.

"Shall we?" she asked Joshua as she looped her hand through the crook of his elbow and ushered him toward Samantha's bus. When they got the door, she knocked and they heard a loud, "Come in." Joshua pulled on the handle to open the door on the bus as Jackson approached from the rear.

"I guess I'm supposed to hang out right here until she goes on stage."

"Sounds good."

They walked inside only to be awed by the glamour and glitz of the massive coach. "Wow."

"You like?"

A tall, leggy blonde stepped out of the back dressed to the nines. She has skin tight jeans, a flowing red blouse, red cowboy boots, and a white cowboy hat sitting on top of her long tresses. "Hey, girl. How are you?"

The two women hugged briefly. "This is my fiancé, Joshua. Joshua, meet Samantha Harris."

"Nice to meet you, ma'am."

"Wow. A real one, eh?"

"Real, ma'am?"

"Cowboy. I don't see too many of those these days. Most are wannabes. Drives me nuts."

"Yes, ma'am. About as real as they come."

"Do you ride rodeo?"

"No ma'am. Too busy on my family's ranch outside Bandera to ride rodeo."

She glanced at Candace with a grin. "Definitely a real one. How'd you find him?"

"It's a long story. One we'll have to talk about some other time."

"Is everything set up?"

"Yep. You'll be on stage at nine for an hour. The opening bands will go before you."

"Good. I have some time then. I don't like to have to rush to be ready."

"Aren't you ready now?"

"Mostly, but I have to psych myself up before I go out there."

"Wow, really?"

"Yeah. I still get stage fright."

Candace grinned. "I suppose I should introduce you to your security guard. He's outside."

"Oh?"

"Yeah, he's also one of eight of Joshua's brothers."

"Eight?"

"Yes, ma'am. We have a big family."

"Apparently." She swept her hand to indicate they should proceed her. "Let's meet this security guy you've got to look out for me."

As they walked outside the bus, Samantha bolted around them to head to the back. "Who the hell are you and what are you doing loitering around my bus? Speak up, cowboy, I don't have all day!"

"Ma'am?"

"Don't ma'am me, cowboy. If you don't have any business being back here, get lost."

"I'm Jackson, ma'am."

"Jackson?"

"Samantha Harris, meet Jackson Young, your security detail."

The End

About the Author

Sandy Sullivan is a romance author, who, when not writing, spends her time with her husband Shaun on their farm in middle Tennessee. She loves to ride her horses, play with their dogs and relax on the porch, enjoying the rolling hills of her home south of Nashville. Country music is a passion of hers and she loves to listen to it while she writes.

She is an avid reader of romance novels and enjoys reading Nora Roberts, Jude Deveraux and Susan Wiggs. Finding new authors and delving into something different helps feed the need for literature. A registered nurse by education, she loves to help people and spread the enjoyment of romance to those around her with her novels. She loves cowboys so you'll find many of her novels have sexy men in tight jeans and cowboy boots.

www.romancestorytime.com

Other books by Sandy

Love Me Once, Love Me Twice (Montana
Cowboys 1)
Before the Night is Over (Montana Cowboys 2)
Two for the Price of One (Montana Cowboys 3)
Difficult Choices (Montana Cowboys 4)
Doctor Me Up (Montana Cowboys 5)
Stakin' His Claim
Country Minded Cougar
Meet Me in the Barn
Taming the Cougar
The Call of Duty Anthology
Five Hearts Anthology
Trouble With a Cowboy
Gotta Love a Cowboy
Make Mine a Cowboy (Cowboy Dreamin' 1)
Healing a Cowboy's Heart (Cowboy Dreamin' 2)
For the Love of a Cowboy (Cowboy Dreamin' 3)
Tempted by the Cowboy (Cowboy Dreamin' 4)
Forever Kind of Cowboy (Cowboy Dreamin' 5)

Secret Cravings Publishing
www.secretcravingspublishing.com